Apollo Salvatoir

Shā-Shŭ the Dragon

龍
之
舞

Hiram J. Bertoch

Editor: Lara Kennedy

Cover Design By Hiram Bertoch

Expert Readers: Devoone Parsons, Dawn Nelson, Anna Bertoch

www.ApolloSalvatoir.com

Library of Congress Control Number: 2022932281

Copyright © 2022 Finny Wiggen Media

10 9 8 7 6 5 4 3 2

ISBN: 978-1-946334-98-5

Imprint: Finny Wiggen Media

Charleston, West Virginia, USA

To Each of my Former Students

I hope that you find your destiny!

You can do hard things!!

The infant sleeping in his mother's arms knows as much about his own future destiny as a fluttering maple seed comprehends the mighty tree that it will one day become.

Hépíng jīngshén

Chapter One

Many stories of the great Shā-Shŭ and his childhood companion have been recorded in other books and scrolls over the past few centuries. Indeed, there are likely enough of these works to fill the lotus rooms of every Dragon Temple on Earth. One might then understandably ask, why write another?

The answer to this question lies in the fact that these histories do not always agree with one another. In the years following the lives of these two transformative figures, It has become increasingly difficult to separate fact from legend. To know where embellishment begins and where the flame of certainty flickers out, becoming lost to the darkness of myth and legend.

—*The Book of the Wyvern Spirits*

On the last day of school, the building at Willoughby's Academy was almost entirely abandoned. Final exams were completed, textbooks were turned in, and students had already cleaned out their lockers. All that was left to do was turn off the lights and lock the front doors. This final day of school would really just be a formality.

There was an unwritten rule within the school's community that none of the students were expected to show up for their classes. As a result, the teachers wouldn't mark anyone absent. If anything, they would be annoyed by those few students who did bother to come in.

In Apollo's case, though, none of that mattered because he didn't have a choice. Unlike other children, he wasn't wanted at home. So if the school doors were open, that was where he would be sent.

Having to go to school on the final day would have annoyed him if it weren't for the fact that it meant he would get to see his best friend one last time before the two of them were separated from each other for summer vacations.

Apollo was startled by how empty the grounds felt as his father's car approached the building, bringing the courtyard into view. There should have been students laughing and chasing one another around the lawn. Instead, the campus was almost entirely deserted.

His driver pulled the car in and circled around the designated student dropoff lane. Once the vehicle came to a stop, Apollo climbed out, thanked his driver, and began walking toward the front doors.

Besides himself, the only other people outside the building were three Asian men and an Asian woman, standing in the shade next to a brick wall outside the school entrance.

It wasn't unusual for older family members to escort younger children to school. Apollo knew they were just dropping off a sibling or perhaps a cousin. However, the fact that all four of them followed his progress across the empty courtyard with their eyes still made him feel self-conscious. So much so that he was relieved when he passed through the front doors and into the school lobby.

The handful of students in the building spent most of the day sitting around talking to each other while the teachers pretty much just ignored them. In the case of Apollo and his best friend, it was Ling who did most of the talking while Apollo sat quietly and listened to her.

They had been best friends since kindergarten, giving them a lot of time to fall into a comfortable routine with each other. Ling had a compulsion that led her to share pretty much every unfiltered thought that came across her mind, whereas Apollo preferred to sit in silence, keeping most of his thoughts to himself. It was an arrangement that worked well for both of them, except today when Ling became unusually quiet during final recess. Oddly, she didn't say anything for several minutes. Then, when she finally did speak, her voice sounded soft and uncertain.

"Will you do something for me? I, er—" Ling scratched her nose and looked away from Apollo. Her cheeks becoming flushed as she followed the flight of a nearby butterfly with her eyes.

"Ling?"

Apollo couldn't recall ever seeing his friend look so nervous. Nor had he had to prompt her to continue speaking before.
She rubbed her hands together and then began to speak again.

"You are going to forget me."

Apollo wasn't sure what Ling meant by "forget" her. How could he forget his best friend?

"I'm not going to forget you. I will be stuck in my room the entire summer with nothing to do."

It frustrated Apollo that Ling was wasting their last few hours together, reminding him how he would spend summer alone. She knew this was a topic he didn't want to think about.

"You have, like, got to get a cell phone, Apollo, or a computer, or something. What are we supposed to do for the next three months? The stupid Tom-Bomb isn't going to let you play or even come over to my house."

Tom-Bomb was the secret code name they used whenever they talked about his father's assistant. Her real name was Jamie Plover, but her attitude toward Apollo had led to the friends giving her a less flattering nickname.

They had started by calling her the Angry Tomato, owing to her red hair and fiery disposition. However, that was too long and was quickly shortened to Angry-Tom, which eventually morphed into Tom-Bomb.

Two months earlier, after Apollo's mother had unexpectedly died in a car accident, his father had left him under the care of Mrs. Plover. Sometimes Apollo wondered if Ling hated her more than he did.

When Apollo had related to Ling the details of how roughly Jamie had treated him following the car accident that had killed his mother and that he had barely escaped from, Ling had become infuriated on his behalf. She'd hugged him tightly, and for the first time since the accident, Apollo had cried.

Apollo and Ling had tried to arrange playdates at their homes during the intervening months, but Jamie absolutely would not allow it. As a result, the only time they saw each other was at Willoughby's Academy, where they attended school together.

"I still think we should poison the Tom-Bomb." Ling giggled. "Or accidentally push her in front of a car."

Apollo rolled his eyes.

"Okay, not murder, then, but it is seriously unfair the way she treats you, and anyway, I am going to go crazy if I have to be alone all summer. Who am I going to talk to?"

Apollo imagined his friend slowly filling up with unspoken words, getting bigger and bigger, until BOOM. She exploded, sentences flying everywhere.

"What's so funny?" she asked, but before Apollo could answer, she continued. "Anyway, I think I have an idea for how we can get rid of the Tom-Bomb."

Ling spent the next several minutes detailing a plan and trying to talk Apollo into carrying it out. When she was done, he shook his head fervently. No, absolutely not. Ling persisted but then once again fell silent.

Apollo wondered what was bothering her. For her to run out of things to say twice in the same day was highly unusual.

After a few moments, Ling turned her head back up and looked at him nervously. "Apollo?" She paused and then held out her hand, offering him her phone.

"Take it. Even if you don't want to use it to get the Tom-Bomb. This way, we can at least still talk to each other. I can text you from my tablet."

Apollo felt uncomfortable taking her phone; however, talking to someone besides himself would be a relief.

Shortly after his mother's death, Jamie had threatened Apollo with physical harm if he left his room. A threat that Apollo was pretty sure she was capable of carrying out. Since then, Apollo had spent his evenings and weekends alone. Cut off from everyone else.

Apollo knew that Ling was right. If he borrowed her phone, he would at least be able to keep in contact with her. Later, he could give it back to Ling when they returned to school in the fall.

"Thank you," he said quietly.

Ling nodded and then reached back into her pocket to retrieve something else. Once again, she extended her hand out toward Apollo. Turning it over so that Apollo could catch the tiny object as she let go.

Apollo examined the object using the light of the afternoon sun. It was about the same size and shape as a quarter but was gold instead of silver. On the front, there were two dragons, whose bodies curled around the outer edge and who were looking into each other's eyes. In the center of the coin, a hole passed all the way through it.

"Um, thanks." Apollo turned it over in his hand. "Is it, like, Chinese money?"

"Look." she said, opening her other hand. "You have one, and I have one. They are a matched set." Ling looked up into Apollo's eyes uncomfortably. "Will you accept it?"

"Yes, but—" Apollo's sentence was cut off by Ling, who unexpectedly leaned in and kissed him on the cheek. Then, after another brief moment of silence, Ling returned to a version of herself, though she now seemed to be stuck in fast-forward mode.

She spent the rest of the afternoon rapidly jumping from topic to topic while Apollo attempted to listen. Neither of them mentioned either the coins or the kiss again.

After school, they left the building for what they both knew would be the final time that year. As they walked alongside each other, Ling stuck something else into Apollo's jacket pocket. He reached down to retrieve it, but she told him to wait until he got home. Apollo reluctantly pulled his hand back up.

"Text me tonight, okay." Ling watched Apollo intently, waiting for him to answer.

Apollo nodded as the two of them crossed the courtyard together. When they had reached the student pickup zone, a car was already waiting for Apollo. He looked at his friend one last time, waved goodbye to her, and then opened the car door so that he could climb inside. Apollo cringed when he realized that Jamie was sitting on the bench beside him.

"Is the fat girl your only friend?" Jamie smirked as the driver pulled away from the school.

"At least she isn't a witch." Apollo whispered the words under his breath, though not quietly enough.

Jamie glowered at him from across the bench, and then reaching up before he could move out of the way, she grabbed his hair and yanked him down toward the seat.

"Did I tell the little mutt that he could speak?" she hissed. Then, letting go of his hair, she brought her hand up and struck Apollo on the back of his head.

"BAD DOG."

Apollo silently glared back at her.

"You think you can talk so disrespectfully to me just because your dad is my employer?" Spit was now flying out of her mouth. "Your father may be my boss, but I have news for you. You are nothing but a dog, and I am your master."

She straightened up in her seat and began to talk in a falsely sweet voice.

"Don't worry." She patted him on the back of his head. "I have all summer to train you."

When they arrived home, Apollo dropped his jacket by the closet door in the vestibule and headed toward his room.

"Hey. Get back here." Jamie demanded.

Apollo stopped and turned around so that he could look at her.

"NOW!" She pointed to the floor.

Apollo crossed the vestibule as slowly as he possibly could, partly hoping to annoy her and partly out of fear for what she planned to do to him when he got to where she was standing.

Jamie shook her head. "You don't leave your jacket sitting in the middle of your father's front entryway. I know it doesn't matter to a gutter pup like you, but important people come here to visit Mr. Salvatoir. Do you want them to see your dirty jacket sitting in the middle of the room?"

Apollo knew the housekeeper would have picked it up just like she always did. At most, it would have sat there for only a few minutes.

"Pick it up and hang it in the closet." Jamie pointed first at the jacket and then at the closet door. She tapped one of her high-heeled shoes against the marble floor as she waited for Apollo to comply with her orders.

Reluctantly, he walked to the jacket, picked it up, and then hung it on a hook inside the closet.

"Now, your dad and I have important work to do. So I don't want to hear anything coming out of your room until September."

Apollo turned and hurried toward the safety of his bedroom. When he was confident he was far enough away, and she wouldn't hear him, he whispered again.

"Witch."

A few hours after finishing dinner in his room, Apollo laid down across the bed and rolled over. It was dark outside, but light was still coming in through the gap under his door, which meant someone was moving around in that part of the house. It was most likely one of the servants since neither his father nor Jamie had any reason to be in that part of the house.

Apollo tried to sleep but couldn't. The prospect of being alone all summer made him feel lonely. He missed his mother and would give anything to have her rescue him. Or even just give him a goodnight kiss. Thinking about his mother made Apollo's heart ache. Thinking about kisses, though, reminded Apollo of his friend Ling.

What had she stuck in his pocket? Apollo jumped out of bed and felt around on the dark bedroom floor for his jacket. He stopped a moment later when he remembered that his coat was hanging up on the other side of the house, in the vestibule closet.

Apollo briefly considered sneaking out to retrieve it but decided to wait. Whatever it was that Ling had given him was safe in his pocket for now. There was no reason to risk being caught out of his room.

Apollo laid back down on his bed and closed his eyes again, ignoring his growing sense of despair. Until he eventually fell into a restless sleep, which was disrupted a few hours later by the sound of distant barking. Probably from one of the trained dogs that patrolled the family's large estate at night.

Apollo again turned his head toward the door. This time the hall lights were off. So too were all the lights he could see out his window, which meant it was now much less likely he would run into anyone.

Apollo rolled out of bed and opened the door to see out into the house, which, thankfully, was empty. He took a slow deep breath and then walked down the hall, past the dining room, and up another hallway.

Apollo's bedroom was located on the back of the house. To get to the vestibule, he would have to walk around the bottom level. However, he could cut this distance in half by taking a shortcut through his father's library, which stretched across the middle of the bottom floor and had doors leading to both the back hallway and the front vestibule.

Without thinking, and despite the fact that the lights in the library were still brightly lit, Apollo walked right out in front of the double-wide doors. His father was standing near a bookshelf on the other side of the room, directly facing Apollo. Jamie was also in the room, but she was standing with her back toward him, looking at a television screen while taking notes. Apollo's father hadn't yet noticed him because he was looking down at his tablet.

Panicked, Apollo quickly slid back toward the wall outside the library in the back hallway. Where he waited in terror, listening for the voice of either his father or Jamie to call out for him, demanding to know why he was out of bed. Instead, after a few moments of silence, Apollo heard his father take a couple of steps and then begin to speak in a voice that sounded bored.

"How did Pellice Industries do today?"

"We are up thirty points."

"And Telscro?"

"Also up, but only by ten."

"Good. Very good. You have certainly proven yourself to be a capable leader."

"Thank you." Jamie sounded giddy.

"Not to mention beautiful. I could just look at you all day. But, I am afraid that it is time for you to go home. We have a lot to do tomorrow."

"Why do you still make me live in my tiny apartment? If you really loved me, William, you would allow me to stay here with you." She sounded pouty but also playful. It made Apollo sick.

"It's such a long drive, and I'll just be coming right back in the morning." She was practically pleading now.

"I know." His father said, sounding irritated. It was clearly a topic he didn't want to discuss. "Jamie, it's still too early. What would the press say if they found out I have another girlfriend so soon after losing my wife? I know exactly what they would say, and it wouldn't be good. No, my dear, not yet. Now, no more talk of you moving in with me. It's time for you to go home."

Apollo heard what sounded like kissing and then more footsteps. Jamie was most likely heading toward the vestibule on the opposite side of the library. Still, Apollo wasn't going to take any chances. He sprinted back toward his bedroom and quietly closed the door behind him.

Collapsing on the floor beside his bed, he stared blankly up at the ceiling. The thought of having Jamie as a stepmother made him want to gag. How could this be happening? How could the world be turning out this way? Apollo had gone from being cherished by his mother to being a prisoner in his own house in only a few months. As if losing his mom and his freedom wasn't punishment enough, now the Tom-Bomb was somehow weaseling her way into their family. Apollo swallowed hard to keep himself from throwing up. He knelt beside his bed, grabbed Ling's phone, and sent her a single text.

"Let's get her. Let's get the Tom-Bomb."

Apollo then unzipped his mattress and tucked Ling's phone deep into the middle where no one else would be able to find it. Then, at last, Apollo laid down and fell into a surprisingly peaceful sleep.

Apollo Salvatoir - Shā-Shǔ the Dragon

Chapter Two

It has been suggested that the Shā-Shŭ was a solemn and thoughtful child who set an example that should be emulated by children everywhere. We will not counter this prevailing belief in our present work. Indeed, it seems more than reasonable to assume that the profound truths he taught during his tenure as the ShI-Dǎoshī must have also been found within his heart even as a child.
—The Book of the Wyvern Spirits

"Yes, Uncle, my Xué is in place, and we are prepared."

"Very good, Tengfei. We should be ready to begin in about a week and a half." Tan Far briefly began sorting through a stack of papers sitting on his desk but then paused.

"Wait just a moment."

"Yes, Shīfù?"

"I want to make sure that you understand how critical, how absolutely imperative it is, that your Xué not kill Mr. Salvatoir or his son until I tell you to do so."

"Of course, Uncle. You do not need to worry. We will not disappoint you."

"I know that you won't. I will send a message when I am ready for you to begin."

"Thank you, Shīfù." Tengfei bowed his head and left.

Tengfei was one of the few people who Tan Far respected. Perhaps it could even be said that he liked him. He may have been young, but he was also intelligent and efficient, unlike many other Xué who depended too much on their strength and not enough on their wit or cleverness.

When Tan Far eventually died, someone would have to take his place as ShI-Dǎoshī. His nephew seemed to be the obvious choice. Tengfei was the only person besides himself who possessed the drive, passion, and intelligence to keep the Order moving toward its destiny, which after years of meticulous planning, was finally about to be realized.

All that was left to do was to visit William Salvatoir and convince the smug little man to send his son Apollo away to a private institution in China for the upcoming school year.

Once the boy was secured, and in their custody, Tan Far would order Tengfei to take care of William Salvatoir, just as he had done with the man's wife several months earlier. Soon after that, the Dragon Order would seize control of the Salvatoir's business empire. Following which, Tan Far would also order his nephew to end Apollo's life.

Once the Salvatoirs were disposed of and Tan Far was in control of their vast financial resources, he would finally be able to leave America and return to his homeland. Where he would again have access to the full strength of his entire Dragon Order rather than just the skeleton crew that he kept in San Francisco.

It would then just be a matter of time until he could propel their little Order from the underbelly of Chinese society onto the larger world stage.

Bringing himself both power and eternal glory in the process.

Apollo, who had been lying on his back, took a pillow out from under his head and put it over his face. Then, he closed his eyes and did his best to reassure himself.

"This is for you, Mom," he whispered.

He then stood and walked across the room toward a small white desk that sat against the wall on the far side of his bedroom. Where he carefully hid Ling's phone behind two books so that only the camera would be exposed.

Grabbing his bedroom door, Apollo flung it open and took a position a few feet out in the hallway. Then, taking a deep breath, he started to scream as loud as he possibly could. His screeching voice echoed back and forth across the empty hallway and out toward the rest of the house. After a few seconds, his throat began to burn. But he didn't care. The pain was worth it.

He took another breath and then continued screaming until, once again, he ran out of air.

The Piedmont Vineyard Estates villa was substantial. For a moment, Apollo worried that he might be too far away for anyone else to hear him. His voice was getting raspy. He didn't know how much longer he would be able to continue.

"WHAT IN THE NAME OF—" Jamie came running down the hall toward him. "WHAT IS WRONG WITH YOU?" she shouted. "Your father," she spat, "is in a meeting with representatives from an important— How dare you. What kind of a lun—"

Apollo stepped back into his room.

"Don't you step away from me, Fido." Jamie stepped closer to Apollo, and using the full force of her entire body; she struck Apollo across his face. It was excruciatingly painful.

"I don't know what kind of sick, demented mental patient stands in front of a door and howls for no reason, but here." She struck him again, this time even harder. "Now you have something to scream about."

"If I hear so much as a whisper coming from this room, I will make it so that you need crutches. And no one is going to waste a penny on crutches for a dog." She turned and walked out, slamming the door behind her.

The next few days were more fun than Apollo could remember having had in months. It wasn't just that he was actively working against the woman who made his life miserable. It was also just nice to be doing something together with his best friend. Somehow, working to trap the Tom-Bomb made him feel like he and Ling were sitting side by side in the same room.

There was another advantage to what they were doing as well. As a result of their project, Jamie had begun to lose much of her ability to frighten Apollo, not because she wasn't still dangerous. If anything, she was more dangerous now than ever. Instead, it was because their plan made Apollo feel like he was the one in control. He was egging her on. Every time she yelled at him, called him names, or mistreated him, Apollo felt as though he had gained another small victory over her.

On the morning of the fifth day, as Jamie brought Apollo his breakfast, he decided to see just how far he could push her. Feeling a sort of recklessness that probably gets people killed, Apollo took the tray of food from Jamie and then, in a condescending voice, demanded, "Excuse me, Ms. Plover, but this food is unacceptable."

He then looked down at his plate with an air of disappointment. "Now, off with you. To the kitchen, and fetch me some real food." He flicked his free hand at her dismissively.

Jamie's reaction was perfect. She first knocked the plate out of Apollo's hand and then stood over him while grinding his single piece of multigrain toast and two apple slices into the carpet with her foot.

"There. Is that better?" she asked. "You can eat that off the floor, and don't plan on any lunch or dinner. You won't be eating again until you learn some respect."

At lunchtime on the following day, Jamie brought Apollo a single brown banana. He looked up at her wanting to say something clever, but he was too hungry to think. So instead, all he managed to say was, "Wow, thank you. A rotten banana for lunch."

Jamie smiled sarcastically and turned to leave but stopped when Apollo called out.

"I drew a picture of you."

Apollo walked to his desk and grabbed a piece of paper that had been lying upside down. On the other side, he had used crayons to draw an overweight woman with messy red hair who was sitting on a broomstick. At the bottom of the page, Apollo had written, *Jamie Plover the Gassy Witch.*

"Do you like it?" he asked.

Using both hands, Jamie grabbed Apollo's shirt, picked him up off the floor, and slammed him into the wall. "You know that all I would have to do is move my hands from your shirt up to your neck." She paused so that she could look him directly in the eyes. "It would be easy. No one would even know that you were dead. I could hang you right here with my bare hands and just feel the life drain out of your floppy, worthless body. And you know what? No one would care. No one would miss you. Because you don't mean anything to anyone."

She slowly moved one of her hands up his chest and rested it against his neck. She squeezed tightly and laughed as Apollo gasped for air. Then, after a few seconds, she let go, allowing him to drop to the floor. She then turned and left without saying anything else.

Apollo spent most of his time over the next few days lying on his bed playing games on Ling's phone. He kept trying to bait his friend with questions that he thought she might respond to, but each time he sent her a message, Ling just answered by saying that she was still working or that she had to finish and that after they got rid of the Tom-Bomb, she would be able to talk to him in person.

On the third day of waiting, as Apollo lay sprawled out across his bed, Jamie opened the door and walked into his room unannounced. She never came between meals. Panicked, Apollo grabbed Ling's phone and flung himself toward the wall stuffing it underneath his pillow.

Jamie shook her head. Apparently delighted by how she had startled him.

"Your father is meeting with a very important reporter tomorrow." Jamie looked down at Apollo. "They will be doing a story about how your family is recovering since the death of your mother. It is important that you are on your best behavior. I will come in to—"

Beep Beep

"—What was that?"

Apollo's heart sank. Ling must have sent him a message. How could he have been so stupid to have turned the phone's volume up? Apollo pretended he hadn't heard anything.

Beep Beep

Stop texting, Ling. Apollo silently pleaded.

Beep Beep

"Get up." Jamie's voice sounded venomous. "Get up right now." Her eyes narrowed.

She reached underneath his pillow and pulled out Ling's phone.

"What is this?" She looked at the phone and then began to read the messages that had just arrived. "Who is 'Ding-O-Ling,' and what do they mean, 'It's finished'?"

Jamie walked over to a chair and sat down. She tapped on the screen. A few seconds later, the sound of Ling's voice began to fill the room.

The blood drained from Apollo's face. This must be what it felt like to be on death row. It would only be a matter of time until someone threw the switch that would end his life.

"Hello, world. My name is Tan Ling. My best friend is Apollo Enrico Salvatoir. He and I thought that you would all like to see how he is being treated by Jamie Plover. Jamie is the woman that Apollo's father hired to take care of him."

After a brief silence, Apollo heard Jamie's voice coming out of the speaker.

"WHAT IS WRONG WITH YOU? Your father is in a meeting with representatives from an important— How dare you. What kind of a lun—"

Jamie's voice cut off for a moment and then continued. "Don't you step away from me, Fido." Apollo heard a slapping sound and instinctively rubbed his face where she had hit him.

For the next ten minutes, the video rolled on and on, each cut depicting a very angry-sounding Jamie Plover abusing the little boy who was currently on the front page of all of the gossip magazines. That same little boy whose car accident and subsequent survival story the media was now fascinated by. Ling had done an excellent job of making Jamie sound like a monster.

When the video concluded, the face of the real Jamie, who was sitting in the same room with him, had turned as red as her hair, and her hands were visibly shaking.

She stood up, walked over to Apollo, and spat, "Your father—"

Apollo couldn't understand the rest of her sentence. She walked out of the room with Ling's phone in her hand, forgetting to close Apollo's bedroom door behind her. Apollo could hear her sputtering nonsensical words as she stammered away from him toward the back staircase.

Two and a half hours later, she came back into Apollo's room. By then, her skin had returned to its normal color, and she was smiling. "Come with me." she demanded.

He was too frightened to do anything other than obey. Apollo stood up and followed at a safe distance behind her. Jamie led him out of his bedroom and down the back hallway. At the end of the hall, she turned and continued across the dining room. From there, they went up the back staircase, which led them toward the third floor, where Apollo's father had his office.

As they entered his dad's office, Apollo mostly kept his head down, not wanting to make eye contact with him. Looking instead at the dark brown hardwood floor that stretched out toward a myriad of bookshelves around the edge of the room. These bookshelves displayed strategically positioned decorations that his father had procured to impress visiting guests. Rare items, such as expensive art pieces, a rock from the moon, and a gun once owned by Abraham Lincoln.

When Apollo did glance up, he realized that his father was seated behind his desk and had his back turned toward them. Ling and her dad were also in the room and were sitting on a large brown leather sofa.

William Salvatoir turned around and signaled Apollo to sit down beside them. Mr. Salvatoir then looked up at Jamie and nodded.

Jamie walked across the room toward a large-screen television mounted on the wall and tapped a few buttons, bringing the screen to life. "Hello, world. My name is Tan Ling. My best friend is Apollo Enrico Salvatoir. He and I thought that you might like to see how he is being treated by Jamie Plover…"

As the video played, both children squirmed uncomfortably in their seats. Eventually, Jamie pressed the pause button, leaving Ling's chubby cheeks centered in the middle of the screen.

After a moment of silence, Ling's father turned toward his daughter and began to yell at her in Chinese. When he paused to breathe, Ling made a sound resembling the squeaking noise a duck might make if a much larger animal accidentally stepped on it. However, Mr. Tan cut her off and continued his tirade.

Apollo wanted to tell Ling how sorry he was, but she wouldn't look up at him. Instead, her eyes, which were now filling with tears, remained fixed on the floor.

After a few minutes, Ling's father looked over at William Savatoir, who appeared to be enjoying the scene. He bowed his head and said, "Mr. Salvatoir, please accept my apology. I promise you that my daughter will be severely punished."

"I expected better from you, Far. You have disappointed me."

Tan Far stood, bowed to Apollo's father, and then gestured for his daughter to follow him out the door. As she left, Ling turned and glanced backward, briefly making eye contact with Apollo before disappearing down the hallway.

Once they were gone, William Salvatoir turned toward Apollo and asked, "Do you have any idea how much damage that video would have done to our reputations?"

"But, Dad."

"How dare you. Do you care at all about our family? You try to shame ME publicly." He slammed one of his hands down on the mahogany desk in front of him, causing its contents to shake violently.

Apollo didn't speak.

His father stood up, walked around the desk, and tapped his son on the chest. "You are never to speak to that, that girl or to her father again. Do you understand? Jamie, please return my son to his room."

Jamie smiled. "Of course, sir."

She grabbed Apollo by the arm and took him back to his room. Once there, Jamie looked at Apollo and smiled, saying, "Congratulations. You just ended your life."

Chapter Three

Asking how the great Shā-Shǔ found his way to his destiny is like asking the sun how it found the horizon, or a river how it found the ocean. There are no answers to these questions other than that this is what was always meant to be.
—*The Book of the Wyvern Spirits*

At times, Tan Far could be ruthless and even brutal, but his training usually helped him retain dominion over his emotions. It was rare for him to lose control completely. His daughter deserved it, though. He likely would have beaten her to death had there not been visitors in the house. She was lucky because she would heal.

Stupid girl. To have everything he had worked for undone by an insolent eleven-year-old child. It infuriated him.

"Meili. Come in here."

A short older woman walked into the room and looked up at him. "Yes, Shīfù?"

"I don't care what you have to do, but you get me an appointment with William Salvatoir's assistant. That young, capricious woman. What's her name?"

"Jamie Plover?"

"Yes, with her."

William Salvatoir had made it clear he wanted nothing more to do with Tan Far after what his daughter had tried to do. The fact that her efforts had ended in a spectacular failure didn't matter. Men like William Salvatoir thrived on their egos. His daughter had attempted a death blow against him. There would be no forgiveness. Not for either of them.

His only option now was to work through the assistant. She was young and naive. He could manipulate her, and if that failed, he would just have to kill them all and do the best he could to salvage as much of the situation as possible. There was too much at stake, and he wasn't going to allow a decade of effort and planning to go to waste when he was so close to achieving his goals.

Tan Far breathed out in frustration.

"And Meili, tell my nephew that he may have to wait a few extra weeks, but to remain ready."

The woman nodded and left.

THUMP

Apollo bounced off the wall and landed on his back near the side of his bed. It had been weeks since he had had any contact with the outside world.

During the first few nights after the discovery of Ling's video Apollo had been genuinely terrified. Expecting to see Jamie waiting in every shadow with some terrible new form of torture to inflict on him. After a few days, though, his fears gave way to extreme boredom. Was that Jamie's plan? To simply kill him with loneliness? Well, if it was, then it was working.

He stood up and got back on his bed to try again. Jumping as high as possible, he kicked himself off the wall and attempted another midair flip.

THUMP

He was getting better. At least this time, he hadn't hit the headboard. His bedroom was much smaller than the gym where he usually practiced. Back before, Jamie canceled all his tumbling lessons.

When Apollo was four years old, while watching the opening ceremonies for the Olympic Games on television, he had complained to his mother that he couldn't see anything because the camera angles kept changing. Without missing a beat, she asked him if he wanted to go and see the Games in person. Together they hopped onto the family's private jet and within a few hours were comfortably situated in a luxury suite at the Princess Daniella Royale, one of the most expensive hotels in London.

It was during this trip that Apollo had discovered his talent for gymnastics. He was fascinated by how the gymnasts' bodies contorted, flipped, and somehow managed to land on a small beam. It looked both terrifying and also exhilarating.

Apollo begged his mother to allow him to try it, and of course, it took only a few minutes for her to give in. A private coach was hired for little Apollo, and over the next six years, he began his journey in the only sport where he had any talent.

Being long and skinny had its advantages. Apollo might look like a string bean, but he could also bend like one. He was more flexible than even most of the girls his age. He wasn't good at the rings or anything that required strength. But when it came to floor routines, there was nobody who could outperform him.

His bedroom wasn't wide enough for him to do more than a few flips before smashing into a wall. But anything was better than lying on the floor all day. Apollo started easy, but as the days with no outside contact wore on, he continued pushing himself, taking on bigger and bigger risks. What did it matter if he got hurt? Maybe then he'd be able to get out of his room. Even if only long enough to go to the hospital.

Apollo quickly mastered jumping off his desk, flipping around in the air, and landing on his feet. But that wasn't much different than starting the same maneuver on the floor. It was just farther to fall. Next, he tried running from the top of his bed, where his pillow was, toward the foot and then leaping off, landing in a roll on the plush carpet. After a few painful misfires, he mastered this move as well. Now his goal was to jump off the wall as they did in movies, flip himself backward, and then land on his feet. Which so far had proven to be impossible.

THUMP

Ouch. Apollo rubbed the side of his face, which he had just smacked for a second time against the wooden headboard of his stately maple bed.

Apollo heard his bedroom door briefly open; then, after a few moments, it closed again. Jamie no longer talked to him at mealtimes. Instead, she simply cracked the door open, tossed his food in, and then shut the door again.

Honestly, the silence was more alarming than her taunting and insults had ever been. If there was anything Apollo had learned from watching nature videos, it was that predators were always quietest right before they pounced.

Apollo didn't bother getting up off the floor. He was hungry, but she never gave him enough to eat, and he knew that whatever she had tossed in wouldn't satisfy him. He figured it would be better to wait for dinner. Then he could combine both meals into one.

Instead, he remained on the carpet between the wall and the edge of his bed. Staring blankly up at the ceiling, willing it to open up so that he could escape and fly away.

After what felt like only a few minutes, Apollo heard his door open again. Confused, he lifted his head and glanced toward the door. His shoulder ached, and his fingers tingled from having laid on his arm for too long. He must have fallen asleep.

As Apollo climbed up off the floor, Jamie walked in through the door. She was dressed in a dark gray skirt, pink leather jacket, and held a matching pink handbag.

"Hey, sweetheart. Want to go on a trip?"

Jamie pursed her lips and then smiled at Apollo.

"We are leaving in ten minutes, dearest. Be ready."

With that, she walked out and closed the door behind her. Apollo could hear her laughter grow softer as she moved farther away from him, down the hallway.

What did she mean, did he want to go on a trip? Apollo felt sick to his stomach. The last time someone had entered his room and invited him to go somewhere, it had been his mother. That trip had ended in her death. He didn't want to go anywhere with Jame. Apollo couldn't breathe.

Before he had time to think or make any sense of what was happening, Jamie returned and grabbed him by the arm—pulling him out into the hallway. Apollo's heart raced as they walked across the house.

When they reached the vestibule, Jamie looked down at him and ordered Apollo to get his jacket.

Nervously his legs carried him into the closet, where he picked up his jacket and quietly pulled it up and over his shoulders. He then returned to where Jamie was waiting.

"Don't look so sad. You are about to have an adventure." She snorted, enjoying every second of her dominion over him. Jamie pulled a pair of darkly tinted sunglasses out of her purse and signaled Apollo to follow her outside.

They walked through the heavy wooden doors of the front entrance and from there into the back seat of a waiting limousine.

"It is an important day. I thought that we should travel in style."

A young Asian man who Apollo had never met before was waiting inside the limousine.

"This is Tengfei. He is going to be traveling with us."

Tengfei smiled and nodded at Apollo.

Jamie looked up at the driver and spoke only one word. "Airport." It was not a request.

"Yes, ma'am," came the driver's reply, and with that, they were off.

Apollo imagined his mother sitting next to him as they drove toward the airport. How many adventures like this had the two of them gone off on together? How many times had she come into his room, without warning, to whisk him away on some unplanned vacation? Just the two of them.

"What is the point of owning a private jet if you don't ever use it?" she had told him.

Apollo imagined his mother sitting between him and Jamie, glaring down at her, jealously protecting him. Jamie wouldn't have been allowed anywhere near Apollo if his mother were still alive. But she was dead, and that meant he was alone.

The car arrived at the airport, and soon the three of them were climbing onto his father's private jet and then sitting down on the plush white leather seats inside.

"You're very quiet." Jamie sounded disappointed. "If someone put me on an airplane, I'd want to know where they were taking me."

Apollo knew that she was just baiting him. In an attempt to use his curiosity as a weapon. He wasn't going to give her that opportunity. So instead, he reached down, put his seat belt on, and then looked out the window.

The man who Jamie had introduced as Tengfei sat down on a long couch located on the far side of the forward section, which was arranged more like a living room/dining room than a traditional airplane cabin.

Jamie sat down behind the dining table, where Apollo's mother used to prefer to sit—seeing that horrible woman in his mother's seat enraged Apollo. However, he didn't say anything. Instead, he returned his attention out the window and focused on the airport employees who were fueling his father's plane.

After a few minutes, the pilot pulled the plane out onto the runway, and before long, they were soaring high above the clouds.

The noise of the engines and the wind blowing across the airplane's fuselage created an almost hypnotic hushing sound, as though the sky were trying to lull them all to sleep. Jamie kicked off her high-heeled shoes, adjusted her chair, and put a pillow up under her neck. After a few minutes, her steady and even breathing told Apollo that she was safely asleep.

Apollo decided that he could risk asking Tengfei the questions he refused to ask Jamie. So he stood up, walked over to where the man was resting, and sat down on the bench beside him.

"Where are we going?" Apollo wasn't sure if the stranger would answer him, but it was worth a try.

"You are a fortunate young man, Apollo. You have been selected to attend an exclusive private school." Tengfei shook the book that he was holding toward Apollo as he spoke.

"Where?"

The man didn't answer. Instead, he smiled, looked back down at his book, and continued reading. Fine. If the man didn't want to tell him anything, that was okay with Apollo. He wasn't going to beg. He could be patient. In the meantime, Apollo decided to use the time to get something to eat.

One nice thing about the family's jet was that Apollo could always count on it being well stocked with food. One of his father's weaknesses was that he loved to eat. Apollo stood up and walked toward the second section of the cabin, where the kitchenette was located. He opened the fridge and was not disappointed.

For weeks he had been living off nothing but toast, bananas, and raw hot dogs. Now finally, he had access to real food, and there was no one to restrain him. First, Apollo gorged himself on ice cream, potato chips, and candy. Then he ate half a cheese platter with crackers and tiny slices of ham. Finally, he moved on to filling the rest of his stomach with a series of microwavable entrees.

When he reached the point where Apollo was pretty sure he would puke if he tried to eat anything else, he went back to his chair and put his seat belt on. Apollo didn't bother cleaning up after himself. If he had been with his mother, Apollo never would have left the kitchenette in such a messy state. But he didn't care to impress Jamie. The thought of her having to clean up after him made Apollo smile.

Comfortable and full, Apollo fell asleep. Several hours later, their plane began to descend. The change in altitude woke Apollo up. They landed briefly and then just as quickly took off again. Once they were airborne, Jamie stood up, stretched, and walked toward the back of the plane. A few minutes later, she returned, wearing an almost wicked smile.

"I hope you enjoyed your last meal."

Jamie then looked at Tengfei. "Keep an eye on the brat." She turned back around and headed toward the small room near the plane's tail, which doubled as a combination office/bedroom.

Apollo stood up on his chair, grabbed one of the soft, furry blankets out of the cupboard above his seat, and sat back down. He adjusted his chair to lie flat and promptly fell back asleep.

When Apollo woke up again, it was dark outside. He looked out the window and squinted, trying as hard as he could to see the ground. All he could see, though, were the flashing lights on the tip of the wings and then absolute blackness below.

After a few more hours, the plane once again landed. The sun was just starting to rise. It was still dark outside, but now instead of black, the darkness had a deep-bluish tint. It occurred to Apollo that it was now Wednesday morning. They had been traveling for an entire day. The plane taxied into a garage, where workers refueled it, after which they took off again.

When they were back in the air, Apollo began to feel hungry. He stood up and walked through the door that separated the front cabin from the kitchenette. It was spotless. Jamie had actually cleaned. Feeling smug and self-satisfied, Apollo opened the fridge.

It was empty.

There wasn't so much as a half-full bottle of ketchup. He ripped open cupboard after cupboard. All the food was gone. Someone had removed every single edible morsel.

Apollo closed the cupboard doors and returned to his seat. His stomach growled. Now that he had eaten an entire meal, his body expected to be fed more.

Once again, the plane began to descend. How many times were they going to land and take off?

Apollo walked past Tengfei, who was asleep and returned to his seat. Hoping to see where they were landing, he Looked out the window. But unfortunately, the only thing around them was a mixture of farmland and wild prairie. The plane briefly flew over some old buildings, and then once again, there was only grass below them.

They traveled for another five or ten minutes and then landed on a large piece of asphalt that Apollo assumed must have been some sort of local airport. Though it didn't look like any airport, he had ever been to before.

The place looked neglected. Alongside the faded gray runway, a dilapidated building reminded Apollo of an old barn he had once seen while driving with his mother. Next to that building, Apollo decided a taller structure must have been a watchtower. As far as he could see, there were no other planes or people anywhere.

Jamie returned to the front of the airplane. Where she opened the outside door and instructed Apollo to follow her, they walked a hundred meters before stopping near an overgrown bit of grass just off to the side of the runway. Jamie turned around and lowered her sunglasses momentarily.

"My, my, my, little Apollo." She put one of her hands on his chest and pushed him down into the grass. She then raised her sunglasses and shook her head, pretending to be sad for him.

"Even in a place as pathetic and forgotten as this, it appears that nobody wants you."

With that, she turned on her heels and walked back toward the airplane. Apollo could hear her snide laughter as she hurried up the steps and closed the airplane door. Before Apollo could stand up, the plane was barreling down the runway. Within a few moments, it took off and disappeared out of sight.

Were they leaving him there by himself?

Tears welled up in his eyes, and despite himself, he lost control. All the fears, disappointments, pain, and everything else he had suppressed came out at once. Since there was no one around to hear him, Apollo didn't bother holding back.

He rolled over onto his side and, with great gasping breaths, cried for his mother to come and rescue him. He called for his father too, but he wouldn't save him. His father had allowed Jamie to bring him there. Then, finally, he cried for Ling. She didn't come either, but then Apollo remembered something.

Ling's present. The little package that she had stuck in his pocket on the last day of school.

Apollo sat up and stuck his hand into the small pocket at his side. The last time anyone had reached into that pocket, it had been Ling. Apollo felt silly for thinking about it that way, but it made him feel connected to her. His hand found the small object she had placed in there a few months earlier. He quickly pulled it out, looked down, and wept again over what he saw.

Chapter Four

Much has been written about the resourcefulness of the great Shā-Shŭ. It has been said that he could find water in the sand or make weapons from leaves. No one can dispute that he had an uncanny ability to survive. How many times does history record his escape from danger? How many stories have been told of his single-handedly defeating armies or of his wrestling a tiger while still a child? Certainly, these can't all be exaggerations.
—The Book of the Wyvern Spirits

Apollo wiped the tears from his eyes and read the note Ling had included in her little gift to him.

Dear Apollo,

Since I probably won't see you on your birthday, I wanted to give you something. I took this candy bar from my dad's store. He won't miss it. You probably won't be getting any presents from anyone else, and I just wanted to make sure that you at least got one from me.

You are my best friend. No one else understands me. I hope you don't mind that I kissed you today. I hope you don't think it was weird or something. I promise I will never do it again. Please don't hate me.

Love, Ling

P.S. If you text me tonight, I will know that you forgive me.

Apollo opened the king-sized candy bar and devoured it. He felt a deep sense of gratitude toward his friend as he did so.

"Thank you, Ling." he gushed out loud with a mouth full of chocolate.

Apollo had discovered her birthday gift late, but he needed it now more than he did on his actual birthday. It tasted so good. Apollo ate every crumb, then licked the inside of the wrapper and finally sucked the chocolate off his fingers. He then reread the note she had written.

Apollo had forgotten about Ling's kiss. It hadn't freaked him out. The exchange had left his mind entirely shortly after it had happened. At the time, he just figured it was Ling being Ling. Full of energy and emotion. After all, it wasn't as though an overly dramatic goodbye was out of character for her.

Ling had ended her note with the words *Love, Ling*. These words now rested heavily on him. Apollo read them a third time and then hugged her letter. Holding it close to his chest while feeling profoundly thankful to know that there was still someone alive in the world who loved him.

Apollo carefully folded Ling's letter and then tucked it back into his jacket pocket. As he did so, his hand brushed across the little coin that Ling had given him. He zipped his pocket back up so that both the letter and the coin would remain secured inside.

Apollo felt a little less miserable, now that his stomach was full of sugar, which restored some of his presence of mind and allowed him to think more clearly.

Jamie was probably just trying to scare him. When she got tired of her game, she would have the pilot fly back around to pick him up. While he waited, Apollo decided to look for something to drink. The chocolate from Ling's candy bar was delicious, but it had made him thirsty.

He looked around and then decided that his best chance for finding a water fountain would be to check inside either of the two dilapidated buildings that stood a few hundred meters away near the beginning of the runway.

As Apollo thought about these buildings, another possibility occurred to him. Hadn't Tengfei mentioned some sort of private school where he would be attending classes this year? If Jamie didn't come back, someone else must be waiting to pick him up. Or, If he couldn't find anyone from the school, he could ask one of the adults who worked in this place to help him figure out what he was supposed to do. Feeling calmer, Apollo stood up and started walking toward the buildings.

As he made his way across the long runway, he was grateful that he didn't have to carry any luggage. The late afternoon air was hot and humid, and he wasn't sure he would have had the strength to carry large suitcases across such a long distance in the sticky heat.

After a few minutes of walking, Apollo reached the first building, which turned out to be an abandoned airplane hangar. The outside of the hangar was covered by rusting sheets of metal that had once been painted red, though most of that paint had long since worn away. There were no bathrooms, vending machines, or electricity. More importantly, there were, unfortunately, no people.

The only light in the hangar flooded in through two massive sliding doors in the front, both of which appeared to have permanently rusted open.

He looked toward the top of the second building, which was encircled by several shattered windows. Instead of a red roof, this one looked like it had once been painted green, though, like the first building, this paint had also mostly faded away. As far as Apollo could tell, neither building had been occupied in years.

He attempted to enter the taller structure, but unfortunately, the only door was rusted shut. Frustrated, he circled the outside of both buildings, hoping to find a parked car. Or even just a road that might give him some sort of an idea where he was supposed to go. Instead, all he found were more overgrown weeds, many of which grew so tall that they extended up above Apollo's head.

The sun was getting low in the sky, creating a sunset that was actually kind of beautiful. Though also terrifying, because it meant that soon everything would get dark. Apollo looked out across the asphalt and then back in the other direction. As far as he could see, he was completely alone. He once again scanned across the sky. His father's airplane was still nowhere to be seen.

Apollo considered his options. He could stay where he was and wait. He didn't have any food or water, but the buildings would offer him protection and shelter. More importantly, if Jamie did return, this was where she would come to look for him.

What if she didn't come back, though? Apollo didn't think he could survive there for very long without something to eat or drink.

Apollo leaned forward onto his toes, trying to see over the grass. He remembered seeing two streets from the airplane just before landing. From the air, these streets had looked mostly uninhabited, but they couldn't be any worse than this place was.

Apollo guessed that he could probably walk to them in an hour or two.

Anyway, if Jamie did return and he wasn't at the airport, this village, or whatever it was, would be the next logical place for her to try to find him. Even better, spending time searching for him would irritate her, which she deserved. In the meantime, he could hopefully find something to eat.

As soon as he settled on this plan, though, Apollo realized he had no idea in which direction the village was located. He couldn't just set off at random. If he did, his chances of finding the buildings he had seen would be practically zero. Instead of ending up at the town, he would get lost and probably starve to death. He imagined his body lying beneath the tall grass where no one would ever find it.

Apollo sat down and leaned his head back against the outer metal wall of the airport watchtower. He closed his eyes for several minutes to clear his mind and calm himself down.

Rather than growing more relaxed, though, he instead began to panic. What if Jamie never did come back? What if she really had left him there to die?

During their flight, she had gone out of her way to hide all of the food from him. What if she had done the same thing here? Leaving him in a place where she knew there was nothing to eat or drink, all alone with no one for hundreds of miles around to help him.

The sunset progressed from yellow to an intense purple and orange, spreading across the entire sky.

Apollo couldn't think. He had felt fear before, but this was different. This somehow felt more tangible.

"Mom, please. Help me. What should I do?"

Apollo opened his eyes and looked up toward the top of the tower. A glint of orange sunlight bounced off one of the broken windows catching his eye. He stood up and inspected the top of the building more closely.

If he could find a way to climb up to those windows, then he might be able to look out and see the town.

Apollo hurried around the tower, returning to the heavy metal door. He pushed on it, but the door still refused to budge. Using the full weight of his body, he shoved harder. Which was enough to make it creak slightly, but otherwise, it didn't move. Apollo backed up about twenty feet and then ran toward the building as fast as he could. When he got close, he jumped up and slammed into the door with his entire body. This time it opened about a foot but then immediately closed again.

Apollo stood up and rubbed his shoulder. Now that he had jostled the door loose, it was much easier to open. Pushing against the door as hard as he could, Apollo was able to create a small gap, which he forced wide enough to allow him to squeeze through. Once he was inside, the door swung closed again, leaving him in complete darkness.

The inside of the tower smelled like oil and dirt. Carefully Apollo waved his hands back and forth, trying his best not to walk into anything.

There was a hole about the size of a baseball, where rust had eaten its way through the outer skin of the building, which allowed a small amount of orange sunlight to filter in toward the bottom of the tower. As Apollo's eyes adjusted, this minuscule amount of sunlight helped him begin to make out some of the details around him.

There wasn't much to see, though. A few old buckets near the door and a large wound-up rope lying in a pile about ten feet away from him. In the center of the room, a ladder led up toward the ceiling. He had expected to find a staircase, not a ladder.

Apollo walked toward the ladder and tested it. It felt sturdy. The metal shell of the building must have protected the wooden rungs, keeping them mostly dry. Apollo had climbed trees before, but never anything this high. The watchtower was at least four or five times taller than his home, which itself was taller than most other houses.

Apollo reached his hand up and began to climb. For a while, the rungs remained solid. However, as he got higher, some of them started to show signs of moisture-related damage, while a few were missing entirely. His mother would never have allowed him to climb something so dangerous. He imagined her voice telling him to turn back.

After several minutes, he began to get sweaty and to breathe heavily. His arms and legs burned from the repeated exertion of pulling himself up step after step.

The higher he went, the more the condition of the rungs continued to deteriorate, making him grow increasingly anxious.

He paused to rest for a moment and to reassure himself. The hole in the wall was now too far below him for its light to be of any help. He could barely see the ladder right in front of him. He had no idea how far he had already climbed or how much higher he still had to go before he reached the top.

Apollo wiped the sweat from his forehead onto his sleeve. Then in an effort to reassert his courage, he pushed up hard off one of the rungs, causing it to break beneath his foot. As he fell, splintering pieces of wood rained down into the darkness below. Fortunately, he was able to hang on with his hands, but his legs now dangled freely.

He struggled for a moment and then realized that he would either have to pull himself up higher or drop his body to the next step down. Going down would be difficult since he couldn't see. Even if he did get lucky and somehow manage to land safely, his weight would probably break that rung as well.

Apollo tried pulling his legs up, but the angle he was hanging from made it impossible for him to arch his back, and his arms were just too tired to lift his weight.

Instead, he kicked off the rails in a fit of panic, causing his body to swing out wildly from the ladder. As he swung back in, Apollo doubled up, hoping to find a step with his feet. Unfortunately, his feet slid between two rungs and then passed up to his knees. At the same time, his fingers came loose, causing Apollo to fall backward, catching himself with his legs so that he now hung upside down.

Shaking, Apollo remained inverted for a few minutes while he caught his breath and calmed his nerves. Then, when he had once again found his courage, he curled his body up and grabbed the next rung above him with his hands. He then pulled himself up and continued to climb.

After ascending another ten or fifteen rungs, Apollo finally bumped his head against the ceiling. Relieved, he reached up and felt along the wood planks for a door or a latch. It took him a moment, but eventually, Apollo found what felt like a groove in the ceiling. Using his fingers, he traced it around behind him and then back together on the opposite side, completing the shape of a square. Relieved, Apollo lifted the door, causing it to open and then fall back onto the platform above.

As the door swung open, a small amount of dim twilight from the now mostly dark sky flooded in through the opening, allowing Apollo to see just how high he had climbed. His ascent had been terrifying enough in total darkness. Now that he could see, it felt so much worse. He swallowed. There was no way that he would have survived had he fallen from that height.

Grabbing hold of the wooden floor above him, Apollo pulled himself up onto his knees and into the large room surrounded by numerous broken windows that he had seen from the ground.

The tower floor felt squishy and mostly unsteady beneath his feet. The wood must have absorbed decades of rainwater. Protecting the ladder's rungs while causing the floor itself to rot. For now, it held his weight, but he was pretty sure if he jumped, he would probably break through.

Underneath the windows, resting across a number of dilapidated countertops, several broken pieces of obsolete technology were covered in layers of bird droppings.

Apollo walked over to one of the windows and carefully looked out across the landscape. Unfortunately, all he could see were hills and overgrown grass extending out to the horizon. Being careful not to fall through the floor, he crossed the room and looked out the windows in the opposite direction. Once again, there was nothing but grass.

The sky was now mostly dark, and the moon was beginning to rise. A windstorm began to ramble across the prairie, shaking the tower, causing it to sway back and forth slightly.

Frustrated, Apollo sat down in an old chair near one of the control panels. The chair's leg broke through the floor as he leaned back, causing Apollo to lose his balance and fall onto the equipment behind him.

For a moment, he thought he was falling through the window. He screamed and flung his arms out to grab on to something. The equipment panel held his weight, though, and after a few seconds, he realized that only his head was outside.

Apollo slid down the counter so that he would once again be safely under the protection of the roof. As he did so, he noticed another trap door on the ceiling above him, which he assumed led to the antenna on top of the structure. Apollo walked over until he was standing underneath it. Even with his arms stretched out, he was still too short to reach the opening.

He walked back and picked up the chair he had been sitting on, which he placed beneath the trap door. He climbed up onto the chair and tried again but was still a few inches too short. He looked around for something else he could use to make himself taller. Nothing in the room stood higher than the chair, but Apollo had an idea. He climbed down and grabbed what looked like an old radio from one of the counters. He carried the radio over and balanced it on top of the chair. He then carefully climbed up onto the radio.

Apollo reached up a third time, trying his best not to wobble back and forth. His fingertips now barely touched the ceiling. Allowing him to maneuver the metal latch off the door so that he could try to push the hatch open. Unfortunately, though, he just wasn't tall enough to apply very much pressure.

Forgetting where he was standing, Apollo jumped toward the door in frustration, throwing his arms up hard. The door popped open and was immediately caught by a gust of wind that flung it backward, slamming the metal door down hard against the roof.

Apollo lost his balance and fell toward the floor. One of his legs crashed through so that it now dangled into the space below. However, his butt landed on a beam attached to the underside of the floor, which kept the rest of him from falling through.

Carefully, Apollo stood the chair back up and again placed the radio on top of it. He then climbed up onto his makeshift stepladder a second time and launched himself toward the opening. He caught the sharp rim of the roof with his hands, and the metal cut into his fingers painfully, but Apollo didn't let go. As he hung from the ceiling, the chair fell backward onto the floor, causing the radio to roll onto its side before tipping through the lower door and crashing into the darkness at the base of the building.

Hanging by his hands, Apollo took another deep breath, and then, using every bit of gymnastic talent he had, he pulled himself up. Straightening out his arms, he rested his stomach and face against the roof. From there, it was a straightforward process to pull his legs up out of the hole. After laying on the steeply pitched roof for a moment, Apollo rolled over onto his back. The rising moon was bright but mostly obscured by the many clouds beginning to fill the sky.

From up here, the building felt incredibly unstable. Apollo could feel it swaying back and forth with the wind. He wondered how long a structure like this could stand. What if all it had been waiting for was some stupid kid to climb on top, knocking it out of the precarious balance that it had maintained for so many years?

Carefully, Apollo stood up and grabbed the antenna, pulling himself higher. The wind seemed to be growing stronger. Though perhaps he was just imagining it. Apollo did his best not to fall as he moved around the roof, keeping at least one hand on the antenna as he circled the top.

It wasn't until Apollo had looked around a second time that he noticed a dim, barely visible light coming from the same direction as a small grove of trees growing near the end of the runway. The light was much farther away and behind the trees, in the same direction as a distant mountain range. Apollo noted the trees and the mountain range. He would use these as reference points when he got back to the ground.

Relieved, he turned back toward the opening in the roof. As he did so, a large gust of wind caught him by surprise, causing Apollo to lose his balance and fall back onto his side. He sat up, startled but not harmed, and slid down the roof, stopping just before reaching the hatch. Where he stuck his head down and looked inside the watchtower, it was darker now and difficult to see much more than just the outline of the room.

Apollo realized he had a problem that he had not considered on his way up to the roof. To get down, he was going to have to jump. Unfortunately, though, just about anywhere he landed would bring with it the very real possibility of breaking through the floor.

After considering his options for a moment, he decided his safest option would be to aim for one of the control panels that ran around the room's outer edge—hoping that these counters would help break his fall. Of course, he would have to be careful not to swing too hard so that he didn't overshoot his target and go out one of the windows, but that was still probably safer than dropping his full weight directly down onto the floor.

Apollo slid down through the hole in the roof and began to swing his body back and forth, doing his best to gauge how much momentum he would need to land where he wanted to. Then, unintentionally closing his eyes, he flung forward and let go of the ceiling.

Apollo pushed backward as his legs smashed down through a desk along the wall, which caused his body to fall onto the tower platform. Thankfully the structure held his weight.

From there, it was an easy enough task to slide across the floor toward the trap door and then down the ladder to the safety of the dirt below.

Once he was back on the ground, Apollo moved toward the outer edge of the building. Keeping one hand against the inner wall until he found the door, which he squeezed his body through—bringing him back out into the darkness of the nighttime air.

Apollo was relieved to be on the ground and outside again; he breathed in deeply and then muttered silently, "Thank you, Mom."

He then took a few steps toward the trees and scanned the horizon behind them. Trying to see the light he had spotted from the roof. However, from the ground, it was no longer visible. Nor could he see the distant mountain range.

He began walking toward the trees, hoping that when he reached beyond them, he would be able to find some other landmark to help him keep moving in the right direction. It was dark, but Apollo figured this would just make it easier for him to see the distant light. He couldn't shake the feeling, though, that there were more dangers in this darkness than he had ever had to face at home.

After taking a few dozen steps, Apollo stopped. About forty feet ahead of him, near the edge of the runway where the asphalt ran into the tall grass, he was pretty sure he had seen something that for a moment had looked like a pair of glowing yellow eyes.

They were gone now, or perhaps he had only imagined them. Either way, the events of the day had, at last, become too much for him. He was exhausted and now also out of courage. He decided to wait until morning when he could set out again under the light of day.

Moving quickly, he retreated back toward the watchtower. Where he practically dove in through the door and slammed it shut behind him. Once inside, he sat down and leaned his back up against the door. He was probably overreacting, but he still felt safer knowing he was leaning up against the only entrance to the building.

Thunder and wind rocked the watchtower throughout the night, which caused the metal door on the roof to repeatedly slam back and forth, banging violently. Water began to pour through the broken windows above and drip down, thoroughly soaking Apollo.

He was miserably cold. It didn't help either that a strong draft blew in around the door where he was sitting. Apollo rubbed his hands together, trying to keep them warm, but it didn't do any good.

The noise from the wind, the trapdoor on the roof, and the thunder eventually lulled Apollo to sleep.

When he woke up, he found himself lying on the ground in a pool of wet mud. Apollo could see a strip of bright blue sky through a gap in the door, which looked warm, sunny, and inviting. He stood up, stretched, and then pushed his way outside.

The runway was now covered in numerous large puddles. Apollo knelt next to one and began to drink. It tasted a little dirty, but he didn't care. It was wonderful. He lifted his head, paused for a few minutes, and then drank again. He was determined to get as much of the water into his body as he could.

When he was full, he splashed some of the water onto his arms and face trying unsuccessfully to clean off the mud and dust that now caked his entire body.

He wasn't thirsty anymore, but his hunger had returned. Apollo looked out toward the tree line and then up at the sky. If Jamie were coming back, she would have done so by now. There was no longer any doubt; he was alone.

With no other options, Apollo stood up and once again began to make his way toward the trees on the distant horizon.

Chapter Five

In his old age, it is recorded that the great Shā-Shǔ often spoke of his love for the hills and valleys surrounding his home village. Perhaps the serenity and beauty of these hallowed grounds gave rise to some of his teachings. It is almost a pity that any pilgrim or tourist making their way to these once-quiet fields is now greeted by monuments, vendors, and crowds, making it very difficult to imagine what these landscapes must have been like during the Shā-Shǔ's own lifetime.

—The Book of the Wyvern Spirits

Several hours had passed since Apollo left the protection of the airfield. So far, all he had found were hills and an occasional grove of trees. Apollo began to wonder if he had only imagined seeing a light from the roof of the tower. Or perhaps, despite his best efforts to walk toward the mountains, he had instead veered off course and had already passed the town.

Another unsettling possibility also occurred to Apollo. What if the light he had seen hadn't come from a town? What if, instead, it had come from the headlights of a vehicle or from an airplane? If that were the case, the direction he was now walking in would be completely wrong. For all he knew, each step he took brought him deeper into an empty wilderness and farther away from help.

He was so hungry. Not to mention dirty, thirsty, and uncomfortable.

He considered returning to the airport, but he doubted that he would be able to find his way, and even if he did, his situation there would still be every bit as hopeless as it was out here. His only real choice was to keep walking and hope he could find someone who could help him.

The grasses around him varied in length, occasionally climbing well over his head. Right now, though, they were down to about the height of his knees.

As the cool morning gradually progressed and gave way to afternoon, the sky changed from blue to a dull gray, and the temperature began to climb.

The mud that covered much of his body helped to keep him from getting sunburned, but it didn't protect him from the heat. He needed to get out of the sun and rest for a while. Apollo spotted a grove of trees growing on top of one of the gently rolling hills and decided that it was as good a place as any to find shade.

When he reached the trees, he discovered that he wasn't the only creature with the idea of using the grove as a place of refuge. A small herd of yaks was resting on the ground in the dust, grunting softly and swishing their tails back and forth.

None of the animals gave any sign that they had noticed Apollo. Instead, they remained comfortably seated in the cool dusty ground as he entered the grove.

The yaks didn't look too threatening in their present state, but they were still much bigger and more powerful than he was. So to be safe, Apollo decided to climb into one of the trees at the edge of the grove.

After sitting down on a lower branch, Apollo thought that as long as he was already in the tree, he might as well climb up higher and take a look around.

As he ascended, he listened to the occasional snorts of the yaks below him, who mostly continued to ignore his presence. Finally, when he reached the point where the branches would no longer hold his weight, he stopped and scanned out across the prairie, trying to find anything that would help him get his bearings.

Apollo cried out, startling a few of the yaks, who now looked up at him disapprovingly. In the direction of the mountain range on the other side of a distant ravine, he could just make out what looked like a tiny blue dot. Apollo didn't know if the small fleck of blue had been the light source he had seen the night before, but the bluish hue was not a natural color. Which meant that whatever was sitting across the ravine must have been placed there by people.

Apollo quickly began to slide back down the tree and was about to jump to the ground, but stopped when he noticed something moving confidently through the grass along the edge of the trees. The unmistakable orange and black stripes of a tiger sauntered along, weaving in and out of the grass. For now, it was too busy watching the yaks to notice Apollo.

He held his breath and attempted to hide behind the thin coverage offered by the branches.

If it hadn't been for Apollo, the tiger's efforts to find a meal probably would have been successful. However, his earlier cry had brought the yaks out of their stupor and put them on alert. When they noticed the tiger, they stood up and began to snort threateningly. One of the larger animals charged toward the tiger sweeping its broad horns back and forth, causing the beast to retreat into the grass, running in the opposite direction away from the ravine.

Hoping the chaos would keep the tiger distracted, Apollo climbed down and ran out of the grove.

He reached a rocky ledge just above the canyon about an hour before dusk. From where he stood, he could no longer see the blue dot, but he was confident that it must be just on the other side of the chasm.

Apollo descended a steep, rocky outcropping and entered into a narrow valley that was several times longer than it was wide. In the basin of this valley, Apollo passed another small group of yaks. This herd included at least a dozen adults and a couple of babies that couldn't have been more than a few weeks old. The yak babies looked helpless as they attempted to run around on their unsteady legs.

Apollo watched them play. They might have been small, but at least they had parents looking out for them. At least they weren't alone.

He took a wide path around the animals before once again continuing forward. Finally, after hiking another half an hour, he had almost reached the ridge on the other side of the ravine. However, to get to the top of the bank, he would first have to walk through a couple of hundred meters of tall grasses growing along the basin and extending up above his head.

The thick grass made it difficult for Apollo to walk or even see very far. Exhausted from the effort of climbing the gentle slope while at the same time having to push his way through the stubborn weeds, he stopped to catch his breath. In the silence, Apollo heard something else breathing behind him.

Turning back and looking over his shoulder, he saw the eyes and teeth of a tiger crouching about a dozen meters behind him. He tried to run, but the weeds were too thick, making it impossible for him to take more than a few steps at a time. On the other hand, the tiger seemed to effortlessly swim through the field, crossing the distance between the two of them with ease.

Apollo fell to the ground, closed his eyes, and buried his face into his knees. For a moment, all he heard was the silent swishing of grass. Then a set of powerful pounding footsteps. Apollo opened his eyes and glanced up just as two enormous horns swooped over his head and crashed into a surprised and now mortally wounded tiger.

A massive Yak continued running toward where the tiger was now rolling in the grass. Then, lifting both of its front legs, it stomped down on the animal, crushing it underneath its massive body. The agitated yak then circled part way around and looked back at Apollo, seemingly trying to decide whether or not the little boy posed any risk to its herd. After a moment, the animal turned and then disappeared into the grass.

Shaking, Apollo stood up and slowly made his way over to the tiger. The animal's eyes were still open, but it wasn't breathing. Apollo kicked it cautiously, and then feeling a little more confident, he kicked it again. This time much harder.

The yak's impact had partially shattered the tiger's jaw, leaving several of its teeth loose. Apollo reached into the animal's still warm mouth and pulled one of these teeth out, slipping it into his jacket pocket. Then, feeling shaken but somehow victorious, he stood up and continued toward the top of the mountain ridge.

The sun was again beginning to set along the horizon, and it was starting to get dark. Apollo had no desire to spend a second night alone in this place, and thankfully it now looked as though he probably wouldn't have to.

A few hundred feet ahead of him, sitting in front of another smaller valley, Apollo could see what appeared to be a well-maintained building with a blue roof. The building looked very similar to the ones Apollo had seen in the Chinatown district of San Francisco. The corners of the roof curved upward with tips that pointed toward the sky. Behind and just to the side of this building stood another similar structure with an orange roof.

Both buildings looked old, but they were in good repair. Someone had trimmed the grass, and each had a small garden near the front door where flowers and vegetables were growing. Apollo raced toward the buildings but then saw something that got him even more excited. There was an entire village behind the houses, hidden inside the little valley.

He looked back and forth, scanning for any signs of life, but couldn't see anyone. There must have been at least five or six hundred buildings sprawled out across the valley, but they were all dark and appeared empty.

As far as he could tell, the various buildings in the village were all arranged along two main roads that crossed each other in the middle. Each of these main streets had several smaller roads that led away from them, spidering out across the rest of the valley. The smaller roads looked more like sidewalks or pathways than proper streets. None of them were wide enough to allow cars to pass through. Not that Apollo could see any cars.

In the center of the village, where the two main roads converged, there was a large square-shaped building which was by far the tallest structure. This enormous building was also the only place where Apollo could see any light.

He tried knocking on some of the doors he passed, but no one answered. Apollo briefly considered breaking into one of the houses to look for something to eat but decided he better not. However, he did reach over one of the fences to help himself to a tomato that was growing in one of the gardens.

As he ate the tomato, Apollo made his way toward the center of town. Every house he passed was virtually identical. The only real difference was in the color of their roofs. Though even that didn't vary much. Some were blue, others orange, while a few were either white or green. There were no address numbers, no decorations, or anything else to signify whose house belonged to whom.

After a half-hour of walking, Apollo eventually reached the central intersection. Where he got his first close-up view of the large building in the middle of town, it was huge. Much larger than it had looked from the ridge above the valley.

The building appeared to be four stories high. Each level was set apart from the one above it by a small perimeter of roofing tiles that circled the entire structure. As the building rose upward, each layer grew slightly smaller, giving the building a very slight pyramid shape.

The roofing tiles that ringed the building between the first and second floors were blue. The next layer of roofing tiles was orange. The third layer was green, and the final layer was white. In between these layers, Apollo could see several windows, many of which were brightly lit from inside.

The light wasn't the only thing coming out of the building. As Apollo got closer, he began to hear shouting and occasional cheering.

The building was full of people. As far as he could tell, every single person who lived in the town must have gathered inside.

Chapter Six

Historians will perhaps always debate how it was that a boy could rise to power so quickly. There are those who believe the Shā-Shŭ took control of his home village the moment he first arrived there and then expanded his influence throughout the rest of the world. Others feel that it was Shi Ju-Long, Jiàn Hui, or perhaps both, who recognized the boy's greatness and who apprenticed him toward his destiny. How it happened, though, is less important than the fact that it did happen.
—The Book of the Wyvern Spirits

Apollo stood outside the opulent building for a few minutes, listening and attempting to make sense of all the noises he heard coming from inside.

He looked around, taking in the building and its surroundings. There was no one else outside, nor were there any signs warning strangers to stay away.

Cautiously he walked toward a porch that ran around the outer edge of the building, which was made out of dark brown highly polished wood and was protected by a large overhanging section of the roof.

On the porch, he found a door with a large dragon bordered by an intricately carved rectangular pattern of repeating flowers connected by a flowing ribbon of gold. The hinges and doorknob were also made out of gold. Apollo ran his hand across the dragon, intrigued by the craftsmanship.

After pushing his way through the door, Apollo found himself standing in a dimly lit foyer located at one of the four corners of the building. The only light in the room came from six candles, each attached to the walls by ornate brass candelabras.

Apollo heard someone shout, followed by a loud cheer. The noise came from behind another door on the wall opposite where he was standing. Like the first door, this one also had a dragon carved into it, which was sitting on a nest, protecting several unhatched eggs beneath it.

Apollo pulled on the door handle, causing it to swing open, revealing a large crowd of people gathered inside. He was about to join them but was stopped before entering the room.

A man placed his hand on Apollo's chest and pushed him backward, signaling three others to join him. They moved Apollo away from the door and out into the middle of the foyer. As they moved back, the door closed, blocking his view of whatever was going on inside.

The man walked behind Apollo and pulled his arms down, causing him to lose his balance and fall to his knees.

"Nǐ zài zhèlǐ zuò shénme?" The man's tone of voice sounded aggressive and accusatory. When he finished talking, he looked at Apollo expectantly, waiting for him to answer. When Apollo didn't say anything, a woman answered for him.

"Wǒ rènwéi tā kěnéng shì měiguó rén. Huízú zhèngzài děngdài dì nàgè."

The man looked at her hesitantly and replied, "Tā yīnggāi zài liǎng tiān qián dào zhèlǐ."

She turned to Apollo and directed herself to him. "Děng tā. Wǒ qù zhǎo huí."

The woman then walked back through the door and into the room filled with people. Apollo tried to follow her, but his arms were still being held behind him, preventing him from standing. A few minutes later, she returned, followed by a middle-aged man who said something to the group that Apollo couldn't understand. The four younger individuals bowed to the older man. Then, letting go of Apollo's arms, they returned through the door and rejoined the crowd, leaving Apollo alone in the foyer with the older man.

The stranger glared down at Apollo, examining him intently while running one of his hands through his hair and then down across the top of his head toward a short black-and-gray ponytail at the back of his head.

He looked as though he would rather be doing anything other than dealing with Apollo. Who suddenly became acutely aware of a small pile of dust that had formed on the otherwise clean floor around him.

After what must have been at least a full minute of silence, the man took a deep breath and then pointed first at Apollo and then back toward the front door. While at the same time speaking to Apollo in a deep and stern-sounding voice. Apollo couldn't understand him, but the message seemed pretty clear. He wanted Apollo to leave the building immediately.

Apollo stood up and nervously kicked one of his feet against the other. Which caused a dried clod of dirt to fall off his shoe and roll across the floor. The man took another deep breath. This time sounding even more frustrated, he once again pointed toward the door and grunted out a single word, which Apollo assumed probably meant "Outside" or "Leave" or something similar.

Under normal circumstances, Apollo would have immediately obeyed anyone as intimidating as the man was. He didn't think it was ever a good idea to contradict irritable, muscular people with dragon tattoos on their biceps. However, Apollo was desperate. He kept his eyes on the floor, and trying very hard to control his emotions, he pointed to his open mouth, hoping that the man would understand that he was asking him for food.

"Please." Apollo begged pathetically. "I haven't eaten hardly anything in two days." A tear dropped down his cheek, leaving a fresh streak on his otherwise dirty face.

The stranger grabbed Apollo by his upper arm and then pulled him through the front door, releasing him only after they were back outside. The man then spoke to Apollo again, pointing toward the marble steps. Apollo wasn't sure if the man wanted him to sit down or if he wanted him to leave. He chose to sit. As soon as he did so, the man shook his head and turned around, returning into the building.

Apollo didn't know if the stranger would get him food or if he was simply leaving him there alone. He decided that even if the man never returned, others would soon have to come outside so that they could return to their homes. If the man wasn't going to help him, maybe somebody else would.

Apollo laid down on the porch, placing his hands over his stomach, which now ached painfully. He had never experienced hunger like this before.

He wondered where his father's airplane was. By now, it had undoubtedly carried Jamie and all his father's snacks, hundreds of miles away. He felt intense hatred toward Jamie. She had taken everything away from him and had left him there completely alone. What kind of person abandons an eleven-year-old boy in a tiger-infested wilderness with absolutely no food or water.

He rolled onto his side and listened to the crickets chirping around him. They weren't alone. They sang to each other. Each one probably had a family who cared about them. They also presumably had food, though Apollo had no idea what crickets actually ate.

With each passing minute, Apollo grew more impatient, wondering if the people inside the building were ever going to come out. In his mind, he imagined the muscular man returning and warning everyone else not to go outside until the dirty American boy on the porch had gone away.

Or perhaps they were all sneaking out through a back door and tiptoeing back into the village, avoiding him. Apollo knew that he was being ridiculous. He could still hear their cheers from inside. But he couldn't help it. He was so hungry, and his hunger made him irrational.

When the noise died down, and the doors finally opened, a young family with two small children walked out. The children seemed amused at the spectacle that Apollo made. He couldn't blame them. He probably looked very out of place with his messy hair, his tattered clothing covered in dried mud, and a layer of dust all over his face and arms. The young mother and father ignored Apollo's pleas for help and walked away, briskly pulling their children along behind them.

Soon dozens of other people also began to stream out through the various doors on all sides of the building.

Apollo raced toward a man walking by himself and attempted to talk to him. But, unfortunately, the man was alone, making it easy for him to hurry away before Apollo could reach him.

An older woman also passed by Apollo. Her advanced age slowed her down, and she was kinder than the others had been. She smiled, but she refused to talk to him just like everyone else. When he spoke to her, she shook her head and then hobbled off down one of the side roads.

After a few more unsuccessful attempts to plead for help, the streets emptied, and eventually, there was no one left. Feeling incredibly discouraged, Apollo sat back down on the steps of the building. Unfortunately, it looked like he would have to spend the night sneaking vegetables out of the villagers' gardens. Stealing wasn't something he would be proud of, but at least he would stay alive.

He stood up and was about to walk down one of the streets when the middle-aged man with the black tunic and dragon tattoo returned. In one hand, he was holding a bowl of something that smelled delicious. In his other hand, he held a cup of water. The man looked at Apollo, shook his head again, and signaled for Apollo to follow him inside.

The stranger led Apollo across the foyer, down a flight of stairs, and into the basement, where the only light Apollo could see came from a few widely spaced candles attached to the wall. The basement resembled the upstairs in almost every detail, except it was darker, and the doors were thinner.

Apollo followed the stranger to the end of a long hallway. The man then led him through a door and into a much more narrow side passageway. As they walked, they passed several wooden doors that lined both sides of the hall. One of which was open.

Apollo followed the man through the open door and into a small room, where a single candle glowed on the wall. The stranger placed the bowl and cup on the ground and gestured for Apollo to help himself. Apollo gratefully sat down by the bowl and began to eat. As he did so, the man left the room and closed the door behind him.

The bowl turned out to have some sort of noodle soup in it, which tasted incredible. After eating his meal, Apollo stood up and looked around the tiny room. It was so small that a full-grown man could have easily touched all four walls at the same time if he stretched out his arms and legs.

There was a thin cushion or mat on the floor next to one of the walls. It couldn't have been more than an inch thick and was barely wide enough for Apollo. On top of the mat, there was a worn-out pillow about the size of the ones on his father's airplane, except that it wasn't as soft. A small blanket was also left for him and was folded neatly beside the pillow.

Apollo checked the door, which he was relieved to discover had been left unlocked. He pulled it open and stuck his head out into the hallway. The stranger must have extinguished all of the candles on his way back upstairs because the passageway was now dark, and Apollo could still smell candle smoke wafting through the air.

Well, at least he was safe. The room was cold and the mattress uncomfortable, but he had a full stomach, he wouldn't get rained on here, and If he stayed the night, then perhaps the man would bring him something to eat again in the morning. Then he could try to explain to the stranger that he was lost and that he was looking for a private school that he was supposed to attend somewhere in the area.

Apollo unfolded the blanket and stretched out across the mat, leaving the candle burning. He wasn't sure how long the flame would last, but he wanted the room to remain light for as long as absolutely possible.

Chapter Seven

Much of how the world now views the childhood companion of the great Shā-Shŭ has been handed down to us by various twenty-first-century historians, who wrote that Ling was loyal toward those she trusted. From these writings, we also learn that she was simultaneously an inspiring and intimidating leader who others feared but were also eager to follow into battle.
—*The Book of the Wyvern Spirits*

Ling had always believed her life to be like that of pretty much any other American girl, except that she was an only child who lived with a single father. Even these details weren't unusual in the San Francisco neighborhood where she had grown up. Ling's father wasn't the only single parent in her community. And there was at least one other girl Ling knew who was also an only child.

Ling didn't get to see her dad as often as she liked. But that was okay. He was busy providing a good life for them. Unfortunately, this meant that he had to spend most of his time either at his deli, *The*

Skinny Pig Grill, or away on business trips. Ling's relationship with her father had never been close, but it wasn't unusually distant either.

He had certainly never been cruel to her before. Which made his behavior on the night they returned home from Apollo's house all the more terrifying. After bringing her upstairs, her dad transformed into someone very different.

His uncontrolled rage seemed to consume his entire body. Erasing any of the patience or tolerance that he had always regarded her with before. The most terrifying thing that evening hadn't been his words or even his physical aggression. What truly had scared her had been his eyes. Now, several days later, the memory of his vague expression still haunted her. Those eyes had looked so hollow and cold. Almost like they were empty.

The more her dad yelled at her, the smaller Ling became. Causing her to retreat to the corner of her bed and pull her knees up to her chest. He told her that she was a stupid, worthless girl and that nobody would ever be able to count on her for anything. He said that she was just like her mother, telling her that her only job had been to befriend Apollo and to get him to trust her.

Ling had no idea what he was talking about. She was Apollo's friend because she loved him. Not because it was her job to be his friend, she tried to explain this to her father through her tears, but he just got angrier, telling her that she was Apollo's friend because he had raised her to be his friend, not because she had chosen this path for herself.

When his anger boiled over, and his words were no longer sufficient to get his point across, he began to beat her. When he was done, she was covered in bruises and could hardly stand. It was terrifying to see him like that. It was like he was a different man. Certainly not the daddy who she had always believed him to be.

For the next several weeks, Ling remained in her bedroom alone. Her world torn apart. Every time the floor creaked, she flinched, afraid that the man who looked like her father but wasn't might return.

While her body worked on healing itself, her mind began to pull itself apart. Had she been wrong to try and help Apollo? Ling felt guilty because she knew that her motives weren't entirely pure. Helping him hadn't been her only goal. She also wanted to impress him. In freeing Apollo from Jamie's abuse, she would have gained his loyalty. Doing something so essential for him would have helped ensure that he would never leave her.

Apollo was too modest to realize how handsome, funny, or kind he was. While other kids sometimes picked on him, it wasn't because he was a loser, as he believed. Instead, she understood that it was because they were envious of him.

She knew that Apollo would realize how special he was at some point, which was something that, as a friend, she did honestly want for him. She even tried to help him by telling him that he was much cooler than he believed.

However, she worried that he would leave her behind when he found his confidence—abandoning her for new and better friends. She knew for a fact that several of the girls in their class had crushes on him, which was evident by how they all watched him. Even the other boys often reached out and invited Apollo to join in their activities. These kinds of invitations were something the other kids never extended to her. No one other than Apollo wanted to be her friend.

Though he didn't yet realize it, when they were older and the time came for him to choose a girlfriend, he was going to have his pick of just about anyone he wanted. Ling hoped that person would be her, but she was chubby, ugly, and obnoxious. So her only chance was to stand by him now while he was still unsure of himself and then hope that he wouldn't forget her down the road.

Now she had ruined everything. If they were ever allowed to talk to each other again, it wouldn't matter. By then, Apollo will have moved on. Her biggest fear since kindergarten had finally become a reality. She had lost her best friend and would now be left alone forever.

Over the years, Ling's father had repeatedly warned her that Apollo was the only child who would ever want to spend any time with her, and of course, he had been right.

Ling looked at herself in her bedroom mirror. She hadn't changed her outfit or brushed her hair in weeks. She was still wearing the same pink pajamas as the night her dad had taken her over to Apollo's house. Her hair was a mess, and she smelled. But she didn't care. She looked how she felt.

She might have taken a moment to clean herself up, though, had she realized that visitors were about to enter her bedroom.

In the early evening, her father and one of his employees from the deli came in through the door. Ling watched her dad. Hoping for some sign of affection, all she saw in her father's face, though, were loathing and contempt.

It was clear that she repulsed him. So much so that he barely even looked at her, turning instead and addressing himself to the man.

"Niu, my daughter is a complete and total failure. She had only one purpose in life, and she let me down." His voice gradually began to rise. As it did, Ling reflexively pulled back and away from him.

"I thought that I would be able to count on my own blood. But it turns out that she inherited the same weakness of sentimentality that destroyed her mother."

Niu remained perfectly still, waiting for Ling's father to finish.

"Because of the failures of this pathetic girl, I will now have to remain here in San Francisco much longer than I had originally planned." Ling's father turned and resentfully glared down at her. "I have no more use for this—this child in my home. I want you to take her back to Xitanxiang. You are to bring her to the Temple, where I want her to begin training immediately."

"Yes, Shīfù Far. Should I arrange for her to prepare to take the Lóng Tiǎozhàn?"

"No. She will not be taking the Lóng Tiǎozhàn. This fat inflexible child wouldn't stand a chance." Ling's father once again glared down at her in disgust.

"Tell Dǎoshī Xiai that she is to take the child exactly the way she is." Niu looked uncomfortable, but he didn't object. Instead, he simply nodded his head in a slight bowing motion, signifying that he would do as he had been ordered.

"Other than skipping the Lóng Tiǎozhàn, though, I want no special treatment for her. She will be three years behind everyone else her age, not to mention that she is lazy and ignorant.

"Nui, I don't want anyone to know that she is my daughter. Her failures would bring shame and dishonor to me and my name. Just tell them that she is an American child and that the ShI-Dǎoshī has his reasons for placing her there."

"Yes, Shīfù."

"I want her gone tonight."

"Yes, Shīfù."

Before leaving the room, Ling's father turned and walked toward Ling. Afraid that he might strike her again, she recoiled away from him, toward the wall.

"You are one of the biggest disappointments of my life, child. I should have you thrown out into the street." Her father paused, looking down at his own hands and then back at her. "You are lucky that you carry some of my blood in your veins. That blood is precious. It means that perhaps if given the right opportunity, you might still make something of yourself."

He turned to walk toward the door but stopped before leaving her room and faced her one last time.

Speaking in a more determined voice, he said, "I don't want to see you ever again. Not unless you can prove that you are worthy of being the daughter of Tan Far.

"It would be better for you to die trying to live up to my reputation than to remain this worthless little girl that you are right now."

With that, Ling's father turned and left her room.

"Come with me, young lady." The man held out his hand but then reconsidered.

"Actually, on second thought, you had better clean yourself up first. I'll wait for you downstairs."

Ling showered, brushed her hair, and put on a clean outfit. She looked around her room, wondering if she should take anything with her. She had no idea where Xitanxiang was, though she assumed it must be in China. From the way her father spoke, it sounded as though she would never again be returning to her home. What would Apollo think when school started and she wasn't there? She wouldn't even get to say goodbye to him.

Thinking about Apollo reminded her of the dìnghūn coins she had shared with him. Of course, he hadn't understood what they meant, but that was okay.

Before leaving her room, she took a necklace out of her jewelry box, opened the chain, and threaded the center of her coin onto it. She then put the necklace around her neck and locked the clasp, allowing the coin to fall over her heart.

She then put on her shoes and walked out of the room, down the stairs, and into the living room, where her escort was waiting for her.

Niu whistled and smiled. "Wow, there really was a pretty girl underneath all of that dirt."

She liked him right away.

He held out his hand, and the two of them walked outside together, where they got into an old beat-up-looking Plymouth Horizon.

"I know she doesn't look like much, but she has been mostly dependable," Niu joked. "As long as there aren't any hills on the way, we'll probably make it to the airport. I hope."

It took Niu and Ling four commercial flights and two full days of travel to get to the Lanzhou Zhongchuan Airport in China's Gansu Province. Throughout the entire trip, Niu made sure Ling was treated like a princess, buying her first-class tickets and anything else she wanted along the way.

From the airport, they took a crowded bus out across the countryside. For the next three hours, they remained cooped up inside the hot and stuffy interior, where there weren't enough seats for everyone. Niu made sure, though, that Ling got to sit and that she was comfortable. He even opened a window behind her so that a breeze would blow down across her face. When another passenger complained about the open window, Niu threatened them with an expression that made it clear they were not to mess with the comfort of the little girl he was protecting. When the bus stopped, they walked a few blocks and then got onto a helicopter. The final hour and a half of their journey were spent cruising at a low altitude across a vast open prairie land until they arrived at the tiny village of Xitanxiang, China.

Niu again held out his hand and escorted Ling off the helicopter. Then, hand in hand, they began walking toward the Temple in the center of the village. Before they arrived, Niu stopped and knelt in front of Ling, looking her in the eyes.

He brushed a ladybug off her cheek and then smiled, doing his best to put her at ease.

"This is not going to be an easy place for you to live, Ling. I am genuinely very sorry that I have to leave you here. You are actually from this village. It is where you were born. But no one here will know that. To them, you will just be an unwelcome stranger who doesn't speak Chinese very well.

"I fear that our short trip together may be your last happy memory for a very long time." He tapped her on the nose. "I shouldn't go against the ShI-Dǎoshī like this, but there is something that I think you deserve to hear."

Niu paused to make sure Ling was listening to him.

"You are not stupid. I don't care what your father has told you. You are a member of our village, and you are a part of us. It will be very hard for you, and you are going to feel all alone. But remember that Niu is your friend and that I will be praying to the Wyvern Spirits for you."

Niu hugged her tightly, kissed her forehead, then stood back up and escorted her the rest of the way toward the large square building in the center of the village.

Chapter Eight

We learn from contemporary news sources and various accounts recorded by historians that as a child, the Shā-Shŭ was well-liked and even respected by his peers. Of course, this is not surprising. His legendary talent for inspiring those around him indeed must have already been blossoming during his early years of training. What is surprising, though, are the accounts recorded in the Temple scrolls, which were written by his peers. They spoke with great awe of how, on his very first day as a Blue Engrow, he entered the Dragon's Nest and single-handedly defeated a great enemy that threatened his entire village. To have witnessed such a miracle as that of seeing a small child defeating a fully-realized Xué must have struck awe and terror into the hearts of all those who were there that day. It is almost certain that no one would have considered treating the Shā-Shŭ with anything less than the greatest of respect after such an event. Of course, it is possible that these accounts have been embellished, but this seems unlikely, considering that the same history has been recorded by multiple people who all claim to have been witnesses.
—The Book of the Wyvern Spirits

"Apollo, honey, wake up.

"Come on, sweetheart, I let you sleep in, but I need your help. We have a lot to do today."

The gentle fingers of his mother's hand ran lovingly through his thick black hair. It felt wonderful to be loved so much and know that he was important to her. Not just important, but the focus of her entire world. To know that he mattered more to his mom than anything else. It made the world safe. Apollo took a long, deep breath.

"Xiànzài. Xiànzài."

Why was his mother speaking gibberish?

"Qǐlái, xiànzài gāi chīfànle."

And why was she talking in such a deep voice?

Apollo could still feel where his mother's fingers had softly raked across his head. He could still feel her kiss on his cheek.

"Qǐchuáng nǐ zhège háo wú jiàzhí dì měiguó rén," the deep voice shouted. This time it was accompanied by a swift kick to his side. Not hard enough to hurt, but not soft either.

For a fleeting moment, Apollo gasped in confusion. Where had his mother gone? Who was kicking him? He opened his eyes and found himself lying on a small mat in what looked like a prison cell. Near the ceiling, there was a square window about twelve inches wide that was too high for Apollo to look through. Not that there would have been anything to see. On the other side of the glass, a stone wall ran upward and out of sight. However, the window did allow some light to enter the room.

"Chuān shàng yīfú," the man barked. `

Confused and somewhat frightened, Apollo rolled onto his side and then sat up. The man was tall, about forty years old, and had powerful-looking arms. As the fog of sleep began to clear from Apollo's mind, he remembered that he had seen the man the night before. It was the same person who had brought him down into the basement and who had left him here in this room.

"Tuō diào nǐ nà xié'è dì měiguó yīfú. Nín huì chuān shàng yīng'ér de yīfú."

The man dropped a bundle of what looked like rags near Apollo's feet. He then turned and left.

Apollo reached out and picked up the bundle. Unfolding the cloth, he discovered a pair of soft, yellowish-white cotton pants, a shirt made of the same material, and a small pair of shorts, which he assumed must be underwear.

The shirt was different from the one the man was wearing. His opened in front. More like a robe. In contrast, Apollo's was sewn together in one piece, with the only openings being for his head, arms, and waist.

Apollo undressed, dropping his dirty clothes into a pile near the foot of his mat. It felt good to peel away the dust, sweat, and grime from his body. Though his hair, arms, and face were still dirty.

Unfortunately, the outfit the man had brought for him was a little too big. The pants hung uncomfortably around his waist, and there was no belt to help secure them. Apollo would have to be careful, or they would fall off. Thankfully, the shirt the man had given him was long enough that it covered up his midsection. So that no one would be able to tell how far down his waist his pants were resting.

Apollo was about to put his shoes back on when the man returned.

"Bǎobèi měiguó hǎo. Nǐ kěyǐ dǎbàn zìjǐ. Gēnzhe wǒ."

"I DON'T UNDERSTAND YOU." Apollo hadn't meant to speak so forcefully, but he was frustrated. As he shouted, he lifted his arms, forgetting about the need to hold up his pants. As a result, the loose-fitting cotton trousers slipped down and fell to his ankles. Thankfully, the cotton shorts fit better and had remained in place. The effect was still humiliating, though. The man burst into laughter. Apollo's ears turned bright red as he hurried to pull his pants back up.

"Wǒ xiǎng nǐ bùnéng dǎbàn zìjǐ. Lái gēn wǒ lái."

The man turned and left, gesturing for Apollo to follow him. The passageway was now much brighter than it had been during the previous night, thanks to the light that shone in through a succession of small windows near the ceiling.

The two walked a short distance until they came to the end of the passageway. From there, the stranger led Apollo to a door that opened up into a busy room filled with several rows of square tables. Apollo was relieved to see numerous children sitting around these tables talking to each other. Some of the children were younger than he was, while others were almost adults.

Somehow, knowing that the people here were responsible for taking care of kids made Apollo feel a little more secure. If other adults trusted these people to care for their children, then it probably meant that whatever this place was, it was at least safe.

Apollo looked around the room. Against the far wall, there was a long, rectangular table filled with food. There was another rectangular table on the opposite side where several serious-looking adults were seated. The room reminded Apollo of the cafeteria at Willoughby's Academy, except that this place was somehow more orderly and quiet. The children were still talking, but their voices were soft, more like the whispers one might expect to hear in a public library than in a room filled with children.

As they walked toward the food table, Apollo could feel the eyes of everyone else following his progress across the room. The children stared at him, and some even leaned away as he passed them.

"Ná yī pán shíwù," the man said, pointing toward the table.

Following his lead, Apollo picked up a small white plate. With his attention focused on collecting his breakfast, Apollo didn't notice the man leave his side until after his dish was full. Then, when he looked up, he discovered that he was alone and everyone was still watching him.

Trying his best to remain calm, he scanned the various tables, looking for an open seat. Spotting one not too far away, Apollo carried his plate of food and hurried toward it. Before he could sit down, though, two of the three children already seated there pulled the empty chair in tight and scowled at him, making it clear that Apollo was not welcome. They looked offended that he would even consider sitting at their table.

Apollo was used to other kids mistreating him. He and Ling had sometimes been picked on at Willoughby's Academy back in California. But, he knew that while other children could sometimes be jerks, the grownups would always step up and protect him.

Apollo glanced toward the table of adults at the back of the room expectantly, but no one came to help him. Instead, they remained in their seats, observing him with the same look of disdain as the children. Confused and unsettled, Apollo scanned the tables again. As far as he could see, there were no other empty chairs available. He looked back toward the seat in front of him and briefly considered trying to pull it out from under the table but decided that probably wasn't a good idea.

With no other options, he turned and walked toward one of the walls. Where he slumped down, crossed his legs, and scooted as far back as possible, trying to become invisible.

Apollo ignored the rest of the room and focused instead on eating his food. A few moments after he began eating, hushed whispers once again gradually began to fill the air. The sounds of the children talking to one another gave Apollo the courage to lift his head and look around. To his great relief, the attention of the other children had turned away from him. Some of the kids concentrated on their breakfast, others on their various conversations, while a few were busy reading.

The children's demeanor was much more disciplined than Apollo was accustomed to. No one seemed to be misbehaving or showing off. Even the youngest children acted perfectly obedient to whatever rules must have governed how one was supposed to act there.

They were still children, though. It was evident to Apollo that there were many friendships and inside jokes. He could see it in the way they interacted with one another, and in the way they smiled at each other. They reminded him a lot of his friendship with Ling.

He missed Ling. If she were here, he wouldn't have had to sit alone. She was the kind of friend who endured things with you. Ling had proven this when she started standing with Apollo in the boys' lunch line at Willoughby's Academy, something she had taken a lot of abuse from the other students for doing. Despite being relentlessly teased, she was there with him every day, and thanks to her, Apollo had never had to eat lunch alone. Here though, not only was he alone, he wasn't even allowed to sit in a chair.

The whispers in the room once again began to quiet down, pulling Apollo out of his thoughts. Had he done something wrong?

Were they looking at him? He glanced around and noticed an older man making his way toward the wall where Apollo was seated. The man's outfit was similar to everyone else's, except his pants and robe were purple. Everyone else wore white pants, and their robes were either green, blue, orange, white, or in the case of most of the adults, black.

As the man crossed the dining room, the children sat up straighter. Even the adults looked at him with awe and reverence. He briefly glanced at Apollo, clearly a bit surprised to see him sitting on the floor against the wall. Then, without pausing, the man turned toward the room and began to speak.

"Zǎoshang hǎo, lóng zhī lù de xuéshēngmen." His voice sounded confident.

"Zǎo ān dàshī jù lóng," the entire room answered in unison.

"Jīntiān, wǒmen nǔlì yǔ wǒmen měi gèrén zhōng de jù lóng hé ér wéi yī." The man's voice was quiet but firm. Everyone in the room sat perfectly still.

"Nín kěyǐ kāishǐ."

The man then walked toward one of the doors in each of the four corners and left. With that, all of the children stood up and assembled themselves into four straight lines, one line forming at each of the room's corners. Then, after a brief pause, these lines filed out through their respective doors.

The adults all stood up and left the room in shorter but equally straight lines, using the same four doors as the children, leaving Apollo alone with an older woman who began to clean up the food and dishes around them.

Hesitating, Apollo slowly stood up. No one told him what he was supposed to do after finishing his breakfast. On the airplane, Tengfei had mentioned to him that he would be attending an exclusive private school. Had he somehow managed to find that institution? Were the children heading to their first-period classes?

Apollo wondered if he should have gotten into one of the lines with the rest of the children. He looked at the older woman, perplexed, but she just ignored him and kept working.

Apollo stood up and began to cross the room toward one of the doors.

"Huí dào zhèlǐ, měiguó bǎobèi." a voice shouted. It was the muscular stranger who had been giving him his orders ever since his arrival the previous evening.

"Lái zhèlǐ ba." the man shouted again. "Nǐ bù huì chuānguò nà shàn mén. Céngjīng. Dǒng nánhái. Gēnzhe wǒ."

"I don't know what you are saying. I don't understand you. I just—"

"Wǒ shuō, gēnsuí wǒ, bǎobèi měiguó."

"Can you . . ." Apollo paused. "Can you just tell me where I am?"

The man turned and walked away, gesturing for Apollo to follow him. They left the dining room using the same door they had entered and retraced their steps down the long hallway and back to the narrow passageway.

The man stopped before reaching Apollo's room and pointed toward a door gesturing for Apollo to go inside alone. Once inside, he found what looked like a toilet, except instead of water beneath the seat, there was a deep hole. It wasn't what Apollo was used to, but it was clean. When he finished, he opened the door and rejoined the man in the passageway.

From there, the man led Apollo back to his room. Once Apollo was inside, the man left, closing the door behind him.

Apollo's clothes and shoes were gone, but everything else was the same.

Barefoot, wearing nothing but uncomfortably loose clothing and completely alone, Apollo laid down across his mat. Having nothing better to do with his time, he eventually rolled over onto his side and went back to sleep.

A few hours later, he was awakened by the sound of his door opening. His prison guard had returned. The man again signaled for Apollo to follow him to the large dining room, where they repeated the same routine as before, except this time, Apollo didn't try to sit down with anyone. Instead, after gathering his food, he went straight over to his place against the wall.

After lunch, the old man in the purple robe spoke to everyone again. When he finished, the children stood up and exited through each of the four doors around the room. Apollo's prison guard then led him first to the bathroom and then back to his jail cell.

In the evening, when the light filtering in through his window began to grow dim, they made a final trip across the basement to the dining room. While he was out to dinner, someone must have attended to his room because when he returned, there was a new candle on the wall, which was lit and glowing brightly. Underneath the candle, someone had stacked a fresh pile of clean clothes next to a small dish filled with scented water.

Apollo undressed and used a sponge from inside the dish to scrub the remaining dirt and sweat off his body. He did his best also to wash his hair, though this proved to be more difficult. When he finished, the scented water was dirty, and the sponge had turned from yellow to brown, but he felt much better.

The three-piece cotton outfit was exactly the same color, material, and size as the one he had just taken off. Once again, the pants were a little too large, but at least they would be comfortable to sleep in. Unlike the previous two nights, when he had been too wet or dirty to sleep well, tonight he would be warm, clean, and dry.

Feeling refreshed and with a full stomach, he lay down on his mat and stared up at the flickering shadows cast across the ceiling by the candlelight.

By now, Jamie was probably all the way back in California and was undoubtedly greeting his father with another disgusting kiss to celebrate getting rid of him. Apollo imagined her taking his mother's place alongside him. Would they have another child? If they did, would that child grow up to be a better son than he had been? Would his dad be proud of him? Apollo imagined the three of them living happily together. Forgetting that they had abandoned him in this jail cell forever.

The next several days were all pretty much the same. Each morning, he was awakened with a swift kick to his ribs and escorted out to the dining room, where he was allowed to eat. He was then taken to the bathroom and returned to his room, where he was left alone. At the end of each evening, someone left him a fresh pile of clothes to wear and a dish filled with scented water along with a clean sponge.

Strangely, the monotony of his days brought Apollo a sense of ill-fitting comfort. No matter how humiliating, a dependable routine is always better than the unknown. Everyone in the building despised him, but at least he knew his place. As long as he stayed against the wall, no one bothered him. He could count on the fact that if he followed the directions of his prison guard, he would eat, sleep, and get clean clothes. Everyone might look down on him, but at least he was safe.

In time this gave Apollo the confidence to begin paying closer attention to his surroundings. As he did, he started to notice things that he had missed during his first few days in the building. For instance, he realized that the colors the children wore weren't random. Instead, each color signified belonging.

When they lined up at the end of each meal, they did so according to their colors, with blues, oranges, greens, and whites lining up and then exiting the same door together. He also realized that a large flower was carved above each of the dining room exits. These flowers were painted the same color as the children's robes who lined up underneath them.

The children who wore blue robes lined up and then exited through a doorway that had a five-petaled blue flower above it. The children with orange robes left using a door with an orange flower. The students who wore green robes exited beneath a green flower, and the children who wore white robes used a door that had a white lily above it, which Apollo recognized because lilies had been his mother's favorite flower.

What fascinated Apollo the most was that everyone who entered the dining room had a nearly identical dragon tattoo on their left arm. Including even the youngest children, who couldn't have been more than seven or eight years old.

These dragon tattoos varied slightly from person to person but were each based on the same basic pattern. Besides Apollo, the only other person without a tattoo was the old woman who cleaned up in the dining room.

As Apollo watched everyone interact, he noticed that the students and adults frequently bowed to each other. Such as, when a child passed an adult, the child always respectfully bowed toward the adult. Likewise, when two children passed each other, the same ritual sometimes also occurred, with one bowing to the other.

The tattoos, colors, and bowing all signified order and belonging. It meant that they were each a part of something and understood their place, whereas Apollo was an outsider who would always be unwelcome there. He didn't have the dragon tattoo, know their language, or wear a colored robe. So, no one in this place would ever regard him as anything other than a prisoner.

Chapter Nine

It has been written that during his early days in the Yuándīng Temple, the great Shā-Shŭ refused to sit at a table during meals, most likely to demonstrate his humility. Showing others that despite his many talents, he did not view himself as being above anyone else. Such wisdom during his youth is genuinely remarkable. Today we take the practice of giving up one's seat at the dinner table for granted. We view it as nothing more than common courtesy for a host to eat their meal on the floor. The fact that this act is now as common as saying "please" and "thank you" makes the gesture seem obvious to us. We forget that during the Shā-Shŭ's childhood, such a thing was absolutely unthinkable.

—The Book of the Wyvern Spirits

Apollo felt like a house plant someone had purchased with good intentions but had forgotten in the trunk of their car. He was withering away in the basement without any sunlight to lift his spirits.

He constantly thought about leaving his room and exploring the village. Of course, he knew that he wouldn't survive out there on his own, but that didn't mean he couldn't just go upstairs and sit on the porch for a while. Or that he couldn't stretch his legs walking up and down some of the village's side roads.

Basking in the sunlight would go a long way toward improving his mood. Afterwhich, Apollo figured he could return to the safety of his tiny jail cell.

So far, the thing that had kept him from attempting this was the sternness of his prison guard. Apollo just didn't know how the man might react if he left his room without permission.

Apollo sometimes convinced himself that the man didn't care where he went. After all, if he didn't want Apollo to leave, wouldn't he lock the door to his room? Yet, every time Apollo checked, it was always unlocked.

This conviction lasted for a while, but then inevitably, he began to question his logic. After all, he was escorted everywhere he went and wasn't even allowed to go to the bathroom by himself. There was also the incident during his first morning when Apollo tried to follow some of the other children out of the dining room, which had earned him a verbal rebuke from the man.

The struggle between Apollo's boredom and fear consumed his mind during his many endless hours alone. Eventually, he decided that the only way to resolve this debate would be to leave his room and see what happened.

More than once, he had decided to do precisely that, only to lose his resolve later. Today was different. He desperately needed to see the sky, which in the end, won out over his fear and uncertainty.

Apollo made his way toward the door, pausing only long enough to adjust his pants, which were sliding dangerously low down his hips. Now that he was finally determined to do it, he was excited.

If he didn't make it to the porch, it would only be because someone had stopped him.

Apollo walked through the narrow passageway toward the main hall and down to the dining room, which was empty. He returned to the hallway and looked around, trying to decide where to go next.

There was a staircase opposite the dining room, which Apollo figured was as good a path as any. Since it went up, and up was where he wanted to go.

The steps were made of white marble, which felt smooth and cool against his bare feet. As he ascended, Apollo ran his hand across the wall, where several blue flowers had been painted, which looked a lot like one of the flowers carved on the ceiling in the dining room. Apollo decided that this must be the staircase the children who wore blue robes used after finishing their meals.

As Apollo continued climbing, the flowers on the wall were gradually replaced by dancing dragons painted in the same pattern and order as the blue flowers had been. Like the flowers, these dragons were also blue. Apollo realized that the flower pattern at the bottom of the stairs hadn't been random. The dragons who had now replaced most of the flowers were positioned to allow them to flow from one dance move to another.

Apollo traced the path of one of these dragons, who appeared to be running forward. A swirling ribbon of gold led from that dragon to another, who was flipping into the air and then to a third, who was landing. The artistry was intricate and beautiful. The artist had outlined each dragon with a golden border and given them each a unique and thoughtful expression.

It seemed strange that someone would hide such exquisite artwork in a dark stairwell. This was the kind of art his father would have used to impress his guests. In the home where Apollo had grown up, paintings like these would have been displayed prominently, where visitors to their villa could have admired them.

As Apollo climbed the steps, the scenes became increasingly intense. The dragons who at the bottom of the stairs had looked playful now began to appear fearsome and angry. What had looked like a dance now began to look more like a battle scene. Even the colors grew more vivid. The single shade of blue at the bottom of the stairs became a variety of intense variations of blue mixed with golden streaks of fire.

The stairs gradually curved around until they reached a single closed door at the top, which was as beautiful and ornate as the walls. The scene of fighting dragons overlapped between the wall and the door, with many of the dragons half-painted on the wall and half-carved into the door.

All of the dragons surrounded a large five-petaled flower carved directly into the center of the door. There was a doorknob in the middle of the flower, made out of gold.

Before opening the door, Apollo turned around and glanced down the stairwell. The eyes of every single dragon as far down as he could see were all looking directly at him. He hadn't noticed it before, but the dragons were painted so that all of them were looking at the same place. Right where he was now standing. It was as though they were guarding the door.

Apollo turned back around and pushed the door open, closing it behind him. Before his eyes could adjust to the brightly lit room, he felt himself flying up against the backside of the door. Someone was holding him tightly against the wall.

"Nín zài zhèlǐ zuò shénme xióngmāo." a child's voice shouted. "Wǒ shuō, nǐ zài zhèlǐ zuò shénme xióngmāo."

Apollo could feel the boy's breath on his face. Whoever was holding him was the same person who was shouting. He sounded as though he couldn't be much older than Apollo. The boy held his forearm against Apollo's neck, making it difficult for him to breathe.

A girl spoke from somewhere behind him.

"Ràng tā zǒu léi. Tā bù zhīdào tā bù yìng gāi zài zhèlǐ."

Her voice was calmer and sounded kind.

The boy holding Apollo up against the wall dropped him, and Apollo fell to the floor. A few of the children in the room laughed.

"Shā-shǔ." the boy said, pointing at Apollo.

"I don't understand you." Apollo gasped, rubbing his neck. It probably didn't matter what Apollo said, though, since as far as he knew, the boy couldn't speak English.

The young man was about the same height as Apollo but had a thicker build. He crouched down in front of Apollo and briskly thumped him on the chest.

"Gerbil." he said. Then, pausing to make sure Apollo understood him, he repeated himself. "shā-shǔ."

Using his knee, the boy pushed Apollo to the floor and applied pressure to Apollo's stomach. The boy laughed as Apollo's face turned blue. Then, he pointed toward Apollo and spoke again, articulating each syllable slowly.

"Shā-shǔ, gerbil." Apollo once again heard a number of the children laugh. Apparently, they found the insult to be funny. The boy picked up Apollo's head and then dropped it down against the floor before standing up, leaving Apollo lying on the ground alone. His head hurt, and he felt sick to his stomach.

"Dài tā huí dào tā de fángjiān." the young man barked, pointing at two girls. They rushed forward, picked up Apollo by his arms, and dragged him backward out of the room.

The two girls handled Apollo easily. Not that he bothered trying to put up a fight. The confidence they exhibited in the way they held him made it clear they knew what they were doing. Getting beat up by the boy was humiliating enough. Apollo didn't have it in him to get beat up by two girls on the same day.

After returning him to his room, one of the girls looked back at Apollo. Then, almost apologetically, she said something in a soft, reassuring voice that Apollo couldn't understand. The other girl rolled her eyes before both of them turned and closed the door behind them, leaving Apollo alone with his thoughts.

He had wondered what would happen if he tried to leave his room. Well, now he knew. Though finding out had been more humiliating and physically painful than Apollo had anticipated.

Chapter Ten

Who hasn't imagined what it must have been like to have lived in the Temple at the time when the great Shā-Shŭ walked its halls and passageways? To have been in the same room with the man who would eventually alter the course of history must have been exhilarating. Standing in his presence surely would have been a humbling experience.

—The Book of the Wyvern Spirits

During his unfortunate trip upstairs, Apollo had been called *shā-shŭ* by the boy who attacked him. If Apollo had understood the boy correctly, *shā-shŭ* meant "gerbil." He almost wished he were a gerbil. Then maybe someone would give him some attention or show him at least a little bit of affection.

Even after attempting to explore the building still, no one came down to check on him, other than at mealtimes. He was simply left alone hour after hour. No one cared if he got an upset stomach, whether he was sick, or if his blanket was warm enough. They fed him, clothed him, and ignored him—their neglected little pet *shā-shŭ*.

None of it made any sense. If this was an exclusive school, as Tengfei had implied, then why weren't they teaching him anything? If it wasn't his school and they didn't want him there, why wouldn't they allow him to leave? And why did they all hate him?

Though, to be fair, not everyone's attitude toward Apollo was entirely negative. There was an exception in the form of a girl about his age who was starting to become his friend. If their brief interactions even qualified as friendship.

Apollo first became aware of the girl during breakfast on the morning following his humiliating experience upstairs when he found himself watching the boy who had beat him up. It angered Apollo to see him sitting so smugly across the room at a table with the same two girls who had escorted Apollo back to his room. Theirs was the only table that had an empty chair. In fact, it was the same table where Apollo had tried to sit down during his first morning in the building.

Apollo watched as the boy smiled and talked to one of the girls. Whatever he was saying seemed to impress her because she first nodded and then laughed. While these two spoke to each other, the other girl turned her head and looked at Apollo, making eye contact.

At first, Apollo felt caught. He hadn't meant for her to discover him staring at their group. But then she did something that put him at ease while at the same time helping to restore some of his dignity. The girl smiled at him. Her expression looked sincere and genuine. Apollo sheepishly smiled back. She held his gaze for a few moments before rejoining the conversation with the other two at her table.

Apollo watched her over the next few days as she entered and left the dining room. He knew it was rude to stare, but he couldn't help himself. He was starved for attention, and her smiles became a source of emotional strength for him.

Sometimes she noticed him, and sometimes she didn't. When she did, she was always kind. She acknowledged him with a nod or a smile, which he then gratefully returned. It wasn't much, but Apollo was thankful to have her friendship even if they had never spoken to each other.

Apollo learned her name by listening to the other kids, who all called her Ai-An. Ai-An brought the sunshine down into the basement for Apollo. Just the fact that there was one person who didn't despise him was enough to keep him from sinking into complete hopelessness. As long as Ai-An was smiling at him, Apollo felt that he still had at least some worth as a person.

With his spirits lifting and his mood improving, virtually every other aspect of his life also began to feel just a little bit brighter. It was amazing the difference a single friend could make.

He found himself wanting to do more than just nap all day. He didn't have any books to read or crafts to work on. But what he did have was his body and his natural talent for gymnastics.

The room they had given him was significantly smaller than his bedroom back home. There wasn't even enough space for him to complete a single cartwheel, which meant that Apollo had to be creative. He tried bouncing from wall to wall, lunging off a corner, catching himself on the opposite wall and then rolling onto his feet. The more he worked at it, the better he became. It was hard work, but it gave him something to do. It kept his mind fresh, and the exercise helped him sleep better at night.

Of course, sleeping better had its drawbacks. It meant that when his prison guard came to collect him for breakfast, Apollo was often even more out of it—leaving him all the more vulnerable to being kicked. Apollo hadn't ever considered, though, that his exercise might make him so sleepy that he could somehow manage to sleep through one of his jailer's attempts to wake him up or that he might miss breakfast as a result.

One morning about three weeks after he had started exercising, Apollo woke up late. He knew right away that he had overslept because his room was too bright for it to be morning. He was hungry, but missing breakfast was a small price to pay for the luxury of having gotten a few extra hours of sleep. Apollo stretched and rolled over onto his side.

He wasn't alone. Startled, Apollo jumped backward, hitting his head against the wall behind him. Resting on the floor a few feet away from him sat his jailer. Apollo looked back at the man for a moment expectantly, but he didn't say anything. Instead, he just kept staring straight forward, with a face that was almost entirely expressionless.

Apollo rubbed his head where he had hit it against the wall and waited for the man to do something. When nothing happened, Apollo considered ignoring him and going back to sleep. Though he wasn't tired, and even if he had been, with his jailer watching him, Apollo didn't think that he would have been able to doze off anyway. Finally, after a few moments of indecisiveness, Apollo sat up on his mat, leaned back against the stone wall of his room, and returned the man's gaze.

The two looked into each other's eyes for two or three minutes in silence. It wasn't long before Apollo began to regret engaging the man in a staring contest. It was agony. Apollo felt self-conscious and wanted to look away. What was the man doing?

Had he come in here just to see how long he could hold eye contact with a child? Was he testing Apollo in some way? Was there something that the man wanted Apollo to do? Apollo knew the rules of a staring competition, and after thinking about breaking eye contact, he decided instead that this was a small victory he was going to take for himself. No matter how uncomfortable he felt, he would not be the first one to look away.

Eventually, his prison guard looked down and began to speak.

"My name is Jiàn Huì." The words were spoken with a nearly perfect English accent. "But you may call me Shīfù Huì. Shīfù means Master."

"YOU SPEAK ENGLISH!" Apollo blurted out. His unexpectedly loud reply clearly annoyed the man who called himself Shīfù Huì, causing him to lean back slightly.

"Of course, I speak English. Everyone here speaks English. It is necessary to—" The man paused and then changed topics.

"Shi Ju-Long has assigned me to be your, er . . . tutor. I will be responsible for teaching you."

"Who is Shi Ju-Long?"

The man must not have been used to being asked questions. He closed his eyes momentarily to gather his patience and then continued.

"He is our leader. You have seen him in the dining room. He is the one who wears the purple gi."

Apollo was about to ask what a gi was, but the man already looked irritated, and the answer was obvious anyway. It had to be what they called the robes that everyone else wore. So instead, Apollo asked a question for which the answer was perhaps even more apparent.

"Wait, everyone here speaks English? Even the children? They all speak English?"

Shīfù Hui didn't bother answering Apollo. Instead, he continued where he had left off.

"You have come to our, er, school to learn. I am your teacher."

"This is a school." Apollo spoke incredulously. His tone made it clear he wasn't asking a question but was instead expressing his disbelief.

"Of course, this is a school."

"Then why can't I go upstairs? Why can't I sit with the other children? Why can't—" The man held up his hand to silence Apollo.

"You will learn what you need to learn when I decide to teach it to you."

The man swallowed and took a deep breath.

"I will expect you to do whatever I ask of you." He looked at Apollo, waiting for him to acknowledge that he had heard this command. "Do you understand? I expect you to obey my instructions."

"Yes," Apollo replied.

"Yes, what?" the man asked.

"Yes, sir?"

"No, don't call me sir. Call me Shīfù Hui."

"Yes, Shīfù Hui."

"That is good," the man said. "But in the future, you will bow your head to me when you speak to me."

Apollo was not going to bow his head. And the man didn't seem too determined to force the point. After a brief pause, he continued.

"Here, take this." He reached his hand out to Apollo and handed him a dark blue book with no writing on the cover. The pages were uneven in the binding, and the edges of the paper were dark yellow.

"You will study this book every day. I expect you to learn everything found inside it, and I will test you when you are finished."

"Shīfù Hui . . ." Apollo looked down, hesitating. Now that the shock of discovering that his jailer could speak English was wearing off, Apollo's mind was starting to form real questions. Questions that he desperately wanted to be answered. "I don't understand. Am I supposed to be here? Did my dad—did he send me to you?"

The man stood up before speaking.

"Apollo Enrico Salvatoir, eleven years old, from San Francisco, California," the man confidently replied. "Yes, of course, you are supposed to be here." He then stepped through the door, leaving Apollo alone.

"Jailer" seemed to be a more fitting title than "teacher." Teachers spoke to their students on the first day of school. They didn't wait several weeks before introducing themselves. Whatever he was, though, Apollo was grateful that he now knew his name. There is a power in knowing someone else's name that makes them feel less terrifying.

Apollo lay down on his mat and opened the book that Shīfù Hui had given him. At least now, he would have something else to do besides just practicing gymnastics. It would be a relief to read something. At this point, Apollo would have been happy with the instruction manual for putting together a riding lawnmower.

Unfortunately, it turned out that this particular book was even less helpful to Apollo than an instruction manual would have been, though. As Apollo flipped through the pages, he discovered that they were all covered in some type of writing that Apollo couldn't read. There were no pictures or diagrams, just line after line of unfamiliar

Chinese characters, like the ones he had seen on the menus in Chinese restaurants. Apollo slammed the book closed and threw it across the room.

How was he supposed to study something that he couldn't even read? What was worse was that the man had warned him that he would be tested on the book's contents.

It was like giving a three-year-old a five-hundred-page book on rocket science and then sternly warning them that if they didn't learn to build a thermonuclear bomb by next Tuesday, they would be in trouble.

Like everything else in this place, it was stupid and unfair. Apollo rolled over onto his side and glared at the book that was now sitting in the corner of the room.

The book might be a complete waste of time, but Apollo had learned something useful from his conversation with Shīfù Hui. The man knew Apollo's name, age, and where he was from even though Apollo hadn't told these things to anyone since his arrival.

Which at least confirmed what Tengfei had told him on the airplane. This was the school where his father had intended to send him. It was a strange and ridiculous school, where they didn't pick students up from the airport, where they locked children in the basement and didn't let them interact with other students. Where the only teacher was a jailer, and the only book was one that he couldn't read. But it was where he was supposed to be.

Knowing this brought Apollo a small measure of comfort. They could neglect and mistreat him. But they couldn't let him die. Not if his father knew where he was, and not if he was paying them to take care of him, which meant that he wasn't as lost in the world as he felt. Apollo finally knew that he wasn't just a beggar or a prisoner.

He was a student enrolled in and belonging to whatever this institution was.

Chapter Eleven

While scholars often write about the influence that Ling had on the Shā-Shŭ, any serious study of his life must also include an examination of his friendship with Ai-An. It is believed that she served as one of his closest advisors throughout his entire life. Some have even speculated that a romance may have existed between them, though there is no evidence to support these claims. What we do know is that Ai-An was kind, thoughtful, and charitable and that the Shā-Shŭ credited her for helping him find his way toward becoming a compassionate and merciful leader.
—The Book of the Wyvern Spirits

"It isn't how others treat you that defines who you are, Apollo. It's how you respond to them that matters. The power to lessen who you are lies only within yourself."

Tayleigh Hartle Salvatoir had spoken these words to her son after he had experienced a particularly rough day at school, thanks to an article in *Celebrity Weekly* magazine. The article, entitled "A Day in the Life of One of America's Wealthiest Families," reported that

Apollo was handsome, confident, funny and that most of the girls in his class were, in the words of the reporter, "rather sweet on him."

Before returning home from school that day, Apollo decided not to tell his mom about how the article had ruined his life. He didn't want to upset her, but also, deep down, he worried that if she knew what kids his age really thought of him, she, too, might somehow look down on him.

Tayleigh was exceptionally perceptive, however, when it came to her son. She had a sixth sense that was, above all else, always attuned to his needs. Regardless of anything else that might have been going on around her, Apollo's welfare was always foremost in her mind.

Which is why the moment he arrived home from school that day and greeted her with his falsely brave smile, her antenna immediately went up. Without a second thought, she set aside the charity dinner she had been working on, dismissed the two women who were helping her, and then rushed to Apollo's side. Scooping him up into her arms and holding him close to her, she asked him question after question until she was sure that Apollo had told her everything.

When he was done telling her about how the article had embarrassed him because he was shy and awkward and never knew what to say to anyone, his mother kissed him on his forehead and did her best to comfort him.

"First of all, my little man, it's okay to be shy. There is nothing wrong with shy people. But just so you know, Apollo, you are not shy. You are quietly confident, which isn't the same thing."

Apollo wasn't sure what the difference was. Whether he was shy or quietly confident, it just seemed like two different ways of calling him awkward. His expression must have betrayed his confusion because his mother continued.

"It's true, Apollo. Unfortunately, shy people don't always know who they are or where they are going, which can sometimes make them easy targets for those who might want to manipulate them." His mother reached down with her hand and wiped a couple of tears out of his eyes.

"You might not always know what to say when you are in a group, but Apollo, you know who you are, and that is what matters. You know what not to say. Knowing what not to say is almost always more important than knowing what to say. Which is what makes you so strong." She softly patted him on his chest.

"I'm not strong, Mom. No one thinks I am strong."

"I think you're strong. Strength is knowing where you stand. Sometimes, Son, it takes more strength not to fit."

"I just want people to like me."

"Apollo, I think you will find that more people like you than you realize."

Apollo shook his head, not believing her. This caused his mother to pull him closer to her and hold him more tightly against her chest.

"Listen to me, bud. We are always much harder on ourselves than anyone else is. I have no doubt that you have more friends than you give yourself credit for, but just so you know, I love you because you are good, not because you are popular.

"It isn't how others treat you that defines who you are, Apollo. It's how you respond to them that matters. The power to lessen who you are lies only within yourself."

Apollo didn't entirely understand what she had meant, but his mother's words had stuck with him, and every so often, they flashed back through his mind. Especially when he was feeling vulnerable, his mother's explanation for what it meant to be strong might not make much sense to him, but the fact that it made sense to her and that she had applied it to him gave Apollo something to hold on to.

Several weeks had passed since the day that Shīfù Hui had given Apollo the only possession he had in his room besides his mat and pillow. The blue book still lay in the corner of his room, exactly where Apollo had tossed it the morning Shīfù Hui had handed it to him. He hadn't touched it a single time since then. What was the point of trying to study a book that he couldn't read?

Since that morning, Shīfù Hui hadn't spoken to Apollo a single time. During the first few days following their conversation, Apollo had tried his best to engage the man in conversation, asking him questions about the school, the village, or anything else that was on his mind. However, when Shīfù Hui refused to answer or even acknowledge he was speaking, Apollo got the hint and gave up.

Since then, things had pretty much returned to the same routine as before, with Shīfù Hui entering Apollo's room in the morning, kicking him to wake him up, and then gesturing for Apollo to follow him out to the dining room.

Apollo did notice that Shīfù Hui's kicks seemed to be getting softer than they had been during his first few weeks of school. Though perhaps he was just growing more accustomed to absorbing them. There were also brief moments when the man appeared to show Apollo kindness, though these moments were rare and ended quickly.

While things seemed to gradually improve between Apollo and Shīfù Hui, they were deteriorating between himself and practically everyone else. The rest of the school now openly mocked him. Calling him shā-shŭ, the nickname given to him by the boy who had beaten him up. Thanks to the cruelty of that boy, everyone now viewed him as nothing more than an insignificant and worthless rodent.

Had it not been for his friendship with Ai-An, he would have been completely miserable. Apollo was grateful that no matter how the rest of the school treated him, he could always at least count on her to smile at him.

The weird thing was that Apollo knew absolutely nothing about her, except for those few things that a person could discover from across a room. For example, he knew that, like him, she was quiet. She didn't talk a lot to the other students. He also knew that she was kind. Her expressions were gracious and patient. Not just to him but with everyone else she interacted with as well.

Whenever they were in the dining room together, Apollo was always aware of her, in the same way someone working in their yard is aware of the position of the sun. He didn't have to look at her very often to feel the warmth of her personality or to know where she was moving. Being so acutely aware of a single person had an unexpected side effect. It helped Apollo unravel a few more subtleties about how the school functioned.

Ai-An was seldom alone, except for a few minutes each evening during dinner, when she disappeared. Otherwise, she was always with the same two people. They entered the dining room together, sat together, and then left together. Apollo learned that the other girl's name was Fānyì, while the boy was named Lei. Apollo burned with anger and hatred every time he thought about how Lei had humiliated him in the room upstairs, then ordered Fānyì and Ai-An to return him to the basement.

Apollo also noticed that it wasn't just Ai-An, Lei, and Fānyì who went everywhere together. All of the students moved together in packs, though most were in groupings of four. As far as Apollo could tell, Ai-An's group was the only one made up of only three students.

Apollo wondered if perhaps this was why the tables were arranged the way they were. At Willoughby's Academy, the same students often sat at the same tables with the same friends, but there had always been some variance.

Here, variance was apparently not tolerated. Every student entered with the same group of kids, sat down together, ate together, and then stood in line and exited together.

Apollo wondered if there had ever been a fourth member in Ai-An's group. Someone who was out for some reason on some kind of an extended vacation.

Lei, Fānyì, and Ai-An all wore blue robes. But Lei had something that the others didn't. On his right arm, he wore a purple band. Only three other students in the dining room wore a similar purple band on their right arms—one for each of the other three groups.

When Apollo realized this, something else clicked into place for him. Several weeks earlier, he had noticed that the students sometimes bowed to each other. He now realized that only these four were being bowed to, which meant that the purple band must have signified that the person wearing them held a position of authority among the other students.

Apollo now realized that in addition to bowing to Lei, the other children in blue robes also followed his lead. When Lei stood up from the table and began walking toward the line of blue students, both Fānyì and Ai-An immediately followed behind him.

Then, as Lei approached the line where the rest of the blue-robed children were standing, they all moved out of his way so that he would have an unobstructed path to the front of the line.

After each meal, Fānyì fell in line behind Lei, and Ai-An took the third position. Lei then inspected the line briefly before turning around and leading the children out the door.

He acted with confidence and authority as though he were one of the teachers. Apollo wondered where he was taking the rest of the kids and what they did once they got there. He imagined Lei standing in front of a classroom, teaching the children how to do math or lecturing them on the lives of the ancient Greeks. If Lei was one of the teachers who instructed the students here, Apollo was grateful that he was not included in their lessons. He would much rather be stuck with Shīfù Hui, even if this meant putting up with his teacher's unpredictable moods.

Such as on this particular morning. After all of the students and adults had left the dining room, Shīfù Hui walked over to where Apollo was sitting. His teacher cautiously folded his arms, and then after a moment of silence, spoke to Apollo.

"I have been called to counsel with Shi Ju-Long. You know the way back to your room, correct?"

Apollo nodded.

Shīfù Hui let out a loud sigh and then raised his eyebrows. "You will go straight back to your room and nowhere else. Do you understand?"

Apollo stood up. Perhaps a little too quickly.

"You mean by myself?

Shīfù Hui didn't answer him immediately. Instead, he looked as though he were trying to decide whether or not Apollo could handle the very simple task of walking through a few hallways by himself.

"Straight to your room." Shīfù Hui repeated the words, this time much more slowly.

Before his jailer could finish speaking, Apollo had already decided that he was going to make as much out of this brief moment of freedom as he absolutely could. He would be obedient in following Shīfù Hui's orders. Right down to the last detail. He would go straight to his room and nowhere else. But he was going to do it on his terms, which to him meant walking as slowly as he possibly could.

Shīfù Hui was still staring at him. Apollo realized that he hadn't yet answered. He bowed his head and spoke in as sincere and innocent-sounding a voice as he could manage. "Yes, Shīfù Hui, I'll go straight to my room."

Apollo then turned and walked toward the dining room exit before Shīfù Hui could change his mind. His teacher remained standing where Apollo had left him—watching every step he took until he was out of sight.

As soon as Apollo was confident that Shīfù Hui could no longer see him, he slowed his pace down significantly. He was still heading toward his room, but at a rate that would take him most of the morning to get there. It felt good to have the freedom to make a decision by himself. Even if that decision was nothing more important than how fast he chose to walk.

Five minutes later, he had managed to move just a few meters when Apollo heard the sound of several simultaneous footsteps coming down the blue staircase. He looked up and saw a group of around sixty children, all wearing blue robes, coming into view.

When they saw Apollo, they altered their course from wherever they had been going and instead gathered around him. Lei stepped toward Apollo and then leaned his face in so that he was only about two inches away.

"What are you doing, Shā-Shŭ? You do not belong in the hall."

Lei pushed Apollo backward. He would have lost his balance and fallen to the floor if he hadn't hit the wall behind him.

"YOU ARE SUPPOSED TO BE IN YOUR ROOM!" Lei stepped toward Apollo as he half spit, half growled his words.

"You will show respect to those who are better than you. When you are asked a question, you will answer it." Lei grabbed Apollo's shirt with both hands and shoved him backward again.

"Why are you out of your room, Shā-Shŭ?"

Apollo's face burned bright red. Instead of answering Lei, he did something that surprised both of them. Apollo brought his knee up and slammed it as hard as he could between Lei's legs.

Lei dropped, doubling over for a few seconds before regaining his composure.

It felt fantastic to take out his frustrations on this bully, though his victory was very brief. Lei was much stronger than Apollo. More importantly, he had the loyalty of dozens of children who were all presently standing around both of them.

Two boys grabbed Apollo's arms and pulled them back, then down, forcing Apollo to kneel.

Fuming with anger, Lei now towered over Apollo.

"It is time for your first lesson in respect, Shā-Shŭ. It is time for you to learn your place."

Lei then said something in Chinese that Apollo couldn't understand. The two boys holding his arms lifted Apollo onto his feet. Before he could catch his balance or protect himself, Lei kicked Apollo hard between his own legs. The boys holding him then let go, causing Apollo to fall to the floor. He was in agony. Physically and emotionally. Lei laughed and then turned and left. The rest of the group followed behind him, leaving Apollo alone on the floor.

Apollo was utterly devastated. Not so much from the physical pain or the humiliation. Of course, these things hurt, but they were pains he had experienced before. He knew that they would pass.

What really bothered him was Ai-An's reaction. She had been in the crowd. Standing quietly off to the side, observing as the other children attacked and then laughed at him.

She hadn't participated. Nor, as far as Apollo knew, had she joined their laughter. But she didn't defend him either, which meant that Ai-An wasn't his ally after all.

Apollo had naively convinced himself that their little interactions counted as friendship. Which led him to believe that if he ever needed someone in this place to stick up for him, she would be there. As it turned out, though, when his back had been pressed up against a wall, she chose to leave him alone.

She was no Ling. Of course, Ling wouldn't have defended him either. She wasn't a fighter, but Ling would have lain on the floor with him, and she would have taken his blows for him if she could.

Unlike Ling, Ai-An was just someone who sometimes smiled at him. She was worse than all the rest of them. They were at least honest in their hatred for him. Her expressions were lies. She spoke friendship with her eyes while demonstrating only betrayal through her actions. Apollo returned to his room alone and fell on his mat, too upset to cry. He felt ashamed of how weak he was. While at the same time angry at everyone else.

Apollo kept his head down during both lunch and dinner, refusing to look up at anyone. He didn't want to see their faces after they had all witnessed him being beaten up a second time by Lei. Most of all, though, he didn't want to see Ai-An.

That night, when Shīfù Hui left Apollo alone in his room after dinner, he undressed and used the wet sponge provided to wash. He then reached for his nightly stack of clean clothing. After slipping on his shorts, Apollo noticed something tucked between the pants and shirt.

It was a piece of paper intricately folded to resemble a small hollow dragon. On the outside of the dragon, there was a short note written in English.

I am sorry that I kept this.
I know it is probably important to you.

Apollo picked up the little paper dragon and shook it. There was something inside. He carefully unfolded two small tabs near the animal's belly, which caused it to open. Once he could see inside, Apollo realized that the paper was the same one Ling had used to write her note to him many months earlier. Inside the dragon, Apollo found the coin that she had also once given him.

Chapter Twelve

Could you or I have hoped to teach the great Shā-Shŭ anything of value? How intimidating such a calling must have been for Jiàn Hui. Late in his life, the Shā-Shŭ wrote that he owed everything he had ever accomplished to his teacher, who, even as a grown man, he still respectfully referred to as Shīfù Hui.
—*The Book of the Wyvern Spirits*

Apollo twisted his body around on his mat to face toward the door. He was miserable and couldn't sleep. Losing the notion of trust that he had felt toward Ai-An had cost him more than just the pretense of having had a friend. It had also cost him his emotional grounding and most of his self-esteem. She had been the only bright spot in this awful place. Her smile had been his anchor. Without it, Apollo once again felt as though he were floating aimlessly alone.

He gave up on exercising and instead alternated between self-pity and restless sleep. This particular night was no different. When Apollo finally did manage to fall asleep, his brain continued berating him in the form of taunting dreams, where he revisited every humiliating experience of his entire life.

The next morning, when Shīfù Hui came in to get him, Apollo was exhausted. His head hurt, and he felt dizzy. Rather than signal for Apollo to follow him, as he usually did, Shīfù Hui instead picked up the blue book from off the floor, and then, while holding the book in his hand, the man sat down on the floor in front of Apollo.

Defiant and miserable, Apollo glared at his teacher.

Shīfù Hui sighed and shook his head slowly. When he spoke, his voice sounded disappointed.

"What have you done with this book since I gave it to you?"

Apollo felt a mix of both anger and embarrassment.

"Shīfù, I looked at it, but I can't understand anything in it. It's written in Chinese. I do everything else you tell me. I eat, I keep myself clean. I go where I am supposed to go." Apollo knew that these were not the answers Shīfù Hui was looking for, but it was all he had.

"Apollo, even an animal eats and keeps itself clean."

Shīfù Hui's words hit a little too close to home.

"You keep me trapped like an animal. The kids all call me shā-shŭ."

"Perhaps then it is true. If everyone treats you like an animal, perhaps you are an animal. Though I had hoped for more from you."

Shīfù Hui lifted the book and handed it back to Apollo.

"Apollo, this book contains everything that you need to be successful here." He paused and then added as an afterthought, "And also to be successful in life. It is a precious gift. Every day when I come in here, I see the book in the corner of your room. Sitting in the same place. You haven't even opened it."

"I opened it."

It wasn't a lie. Apollo had opened it. Once, for about ten seconds. Before throwing it at the wall. Apollo realized how careless it had been to leave the book in the same position. He should have at least had the good sense to move it around the room from time to time. Leaving it in the same place had made it too obvious that he was completely ignoring Shīfù Hui's counsel to study its teachings.

"Apollo, the feet of a dragon stand firm against evil, walking toward and never away from duty."

"I am not a dragon. I am a gerbil," Apollo muttered under his breath.

"You are whatever you decide to be."

Still sounding disappointed, Shīfù Hui stood up and gestured for Apollo to follow him out to the dining room.

After breakfast, Apollo sat alone in his room, contemplating the words that Shīfù Hui had spoken to him.

What did his teacher mean that everything he needed was inside the blue book? Apollo picked it up and scanned through the pages a second time.

The words were still all written in Chinese. Just as before, there weren't any pictures to help him understand their meaning. What good is a book that contains everything you need to be successful if that book is entirely unreadable?

Apollo sat the book back down, this time being more careful not to throw it. Instead, gently placing it between the wall and his small pillow. He then laid down and thought about something else that Shīfù Hui had said. Apollo tried to remember how his teacher had phrased the strange sentence.

"The feet of a dragon stand firm against evil, walking toward and never away from duty."

Over the past few months, Apollo had seen a lot of dragons. Ling's coin, the blue hallway, the tattoos on everyone's arms. It really shouldn't surprise him that Shīfù Hui was now also talking about dragons, even if his comments had only been about the feet of these mythical creatures.

After picking up his food at lunch, Apollo made his way across the dining room toward the wall. As he walked, he could see Ai-An following his progress with her eyes. Apollo didn't care. He was absolutely not going to look at her.

He took a few small bites, then leaned his head back against the wall, returning in his mind to what Shīfù Hui had said about a dragon's feet and their duty. He imagined the disembodied feet of a dragon walking around, making large footprints in the mud, and wondered what responsibilities a dragon could possibly have? Weren't they just selfish creatures who collected treasure and hurt people?

There was, of course, someone in the room who fit that description perfectly. Apollo looked over at Lei, being careful to avoid eye contact with Ai-An. Apollo loathed Lei. If anyone was a "dragon," it was him. Lei was vicious, mean, and powerful. One of the younger students approached the boy and bowed to him. It made Apollo sick. Lei was the most undeserving person in the world to be given that kind of respect.

Then there was Ai-An. She was a different and much more deceptive type of dragon. One who pretends to be your friend so that she can betray you later. He involuntarily glanced toward her. She was still looking at him, and her eyes were puffy and red. Apollo looked away. No. Ai-An did not get to be sorry for abandoning him. What she did was unforgivable.

Shi Ju-Long entered the dining room wearing his usual purple robe. Immediately, everyone in the room fell silent. Apollo could not understand the old man's words, but his confident tone had become familiar.

After Shi Ju-Long finished his mealtime speech, the children in the room stood up and began making their way toward their various lines. On her way toward the blue line, Ai-An intentionally swung around the edge of the room so that she would pass right by the wall where Apollo was sitting. She was followed by Fānyì and Lei. When Ai-An was close enough to Apollo so that he could hear her, she spoke to him.

"Shā-Shǔ, I'm sorry. I was just doing my duty."

She didn't stop or even look at him. To anyone else, it would have seemed as though she had just walked past him.

Ai-An did draw attention to herself, but not because anyone noticed her speaking to Apollo. Instead, the children wearing blue robes all watched her in shock, probably because she was leading Lei rather than following him. Lei was fuming and looked furious. Fānyì followed a short distance behind Lei and also looked affronted.

Ai-An's comment about doing her duty infuriated Apollo. How could leaving someone alone in their time of need be her duty?

Despite his anger, Apollo still found something to lift his spirits, though. When she had spoken to him, Ai-An had used the name Shā-Shǔ. Not as an insult or to make fun of him, but as though it were his given name. Did anyone else besides Shīfù Hui know that his name was Apollo?

The nickname that Lei had given him had come to define how Apollo felt about himself. It made him feel small and inconsequential. But when Ai-An used it, she had done so without malice. Instead, she had called him Shā-Shǔ while trying to ask him for forgiveness. Her voice had been sincere, and she had spoken the name with affection.

Later that evening, as Apollo thought about this, his mind again returned to his mother's words. With the perspective of Ai-An's tone of voice still in his mind, Apollo wondered if perhaps he was starting to understand what his mother had meant about the nature of strength.

When she told him that the power to define his character lay only within himself and that no one else could do anything to lessen his worth, Apollo realized that she probably hadn't meant that another person couldn't insult him. Because obviously, that wasn't true. Apollo wondered if, instead, what she had been trying to teach him was that no one else, other than himself, could make an insult stick. He couldn't stop the other children from calling him Shā-Shŭ, but perhaps he could decide how this name would affect him.

Apollo was still angry at Ai-An, but she had managed to erase some of his pain and to ease his burden a little bit. He wasn't ready to forgive her, but Apollo found that feeding his resentment toward Ai-An now took more effort on his part. In his darkest moment, Ai-An had helped him feel closer to his mother, which was something for which he couldn't help but feel gratitude.

Chapter Thirteen

**Any comparisons between the *Shā-Shǔ and Ling are
challenging, especially when trying to determine which of the two
was the greater warrior. On the one hand, Ling likely had more raw
talent, skill, and agility. On the other, as has been well documented,
the Shā-Shǔ was blessed by the Wyvern Spirits with strength,
cleverness, and the ability to use his surroundings to his advantage.
Thus, it is not unreasonable to suppose that Ling probably would
have had more success when it came to battling inside the Dragon's
Nest, where the rules were clear and where the fighting tended to be
more predictable. Whereas the Shā-Shǔ would have undoubtedly
dominated a battle fought outside the nest, where the only rules were
those of chaos and where unpredictability reigned.***
—*The Book of the Wyvern Spirits*

In the four months since being dropped off by Niu at the
Xitanxiang Temple, Ling had hardly made any progress at all. Before
leaving her with Dǎoshī Cài Xiai, Niu had cautioned Ling that her life
there would be difficult. If anything, this warning had proven to be

an understatement. There were just too many things that her childhood in America hadn't prepared her for.

The rest of the children who lived in the Temple had all grown up in the village. So they understood the way of things in this place. Whereas for Ling, everything was new and different.

As a result, she felt like she was wandering through each day in a state of perpetual confusion. She had been raised with computers, cell phones, and minimal discipline. While the rest of the children in her Leheqi didn't know what electricity was and lived by a code of strict adherence to rules.

For the time being, her biggest obstacle was language. Everyone else in the Temple preferred to speak Chinese. They spoke English, but only when they had to. As a result, communicating with Ling brought inherent displeasure. When they conversed among themselves, it was always in Chinese, which meant that Ling was often left out of their conversations. She could communicate in Chinese, but not very well. She understood much of what the other children said, but when she tried to speak back to them, she felt like a toddler, saying things incorrectly or using the wrong words.

Before leaving her there, Niu had explained to Cài Xiai that he was acting under the orders of the ShI-Dǎoshī. Who commanded that the girl be trained up as a Dragon. Niu informed the Dǎoshī that even though she was already eleven years old, the little girl had no knowledge of the Dragon's Dance, the Dragon's Creed, or any of their other traditions.

Dǎoshī Xiai's outrage was evident. She exuded indignation through both her body language and expressions. However, she didn't state this outrage out loud. Instead, she told Niu to report to the ShI-Dǎoshī that she would carry out his orders immediately. Niu bowed to Dăoshī Xiai, and then, after smiling one last time at Ling, he turned and walked out the door, leaving her in the Temple.

Once they were alone, Dăoshī Xiai instructed Ling to follow her deeper into the building. She led Ling down a wide hallway and into a room located in one of the four corners on the main level of the building.

The room had blue walls and a large painting of a four-headed dragon on the ceiling. As they entered, several children about the same age as Ling immediately fell silent and lined up, forming four straight rows. Something Ling later learned was the expected behavior whenever the Dăoshī entered into any part of the Temple.

The Dăoshī then spoke to the children in English.

"We have been asked by the ShI-Dăoshī himself to take this fat American girl into our nest and to train her up as a Dragon." Some of the children looked at Ling, confused.

"My guess is that she probably can't even bend down to touch her toes, nor does she know anything about our ways. It will therefore be important that all of you help her learn what is expected of a Dragon." The Dăoshī smiled dryly as she looked back at Ling. "Every time she makes a mistake, no matter how small that mistake might be, it will bring dishonor upon your entire Leheqi.

"Do you want your Leheqi to be dishonored by this ridiculous American girl?" Dăoshī Xiai looked around the room and made eye contact with several of the children, who emphatically shook their heads back and forth. "Good, then it will be up to each of you to restore your honor by correcting her whenever she does something wrong.

"No matter how small her errors are, you have permission to punish her in any way that you see fit until she learns how to behave properly."

Dǎoshī Xiai then looked at a girl with a purple band around her right arm. She was about the same age as Ling, though taller and more self-assured. "Qiao, as you are Qiān-lóng of your Leheqi, I will leave the girl's training in your hands. If she fails, I will hold you personally responsible. Do you understand?"

"Yes, Shīfù." The girl bowed her head.

"Good, then I am going to assign her to your Xué."

Qiao looked horrified.

"Which means that we will need to make a slight adjustment, won't we? Let's see. Yes. Gāo Song, you will no longer be training as a Dragon. The ShI-Dǎoshī has decided that this unworthy American girl should have a place in our Temple, and that place is the one you used to occupy. You will return to the village tonight and will be assigned to work alongside your parents in the crop fields. This worthless girl will take possession of your room, your clothes, and your books."

There were audible gasps all around the room. Ling later learned that no one had ever been dismissed like that from the Dragon's Nest before. Once someone earned the right to train as a Dragon, it was supposed to be a lifelong appointment. Gāo Song's return to his home would bring tremendous dishonor to him and his family. Something the other children in her Leheqi were determined would not happen to them.

The Dǎoshī's had permitted them to punish her, and they did so liberally. This meant that Ling was now the frequent recipient of what the children called "blessings," but which felt more like abuse to Ling. Whenever she accidentally stepped out of line or did anything that she wasn't supposed to do, someone was always close by to "bless" her in the name of restoring their honor.

By the end of her first month, she learned how to behave in the halls and dining room, when to get her food, and to whom she was expected to bow. In these parts of the Temple, she soon began to look and act just like any other Blue Engrow, except, of course, for the fact that she was chubbier than the rest of them.

Unfortunately, though, they only spent a small amount of time in other parts of the Temple. The children spent most of their day inside the Blue Engrow training room or in the Dragon's Nest. In either of these places, it was impossible for her to fit in.

The other children had been training since their infancy. They were flexible, strong, and fast, unlike Ling, who, as it turned out, really couldn't touch her toes. Watching television and hanging out with Apollo her entire life hadn't prepared her to perform the advanced forms and maneuvers that the other children could all do with ease.

Many things about her life in the Temple were hard, but the thing she hated the most was when they had to spar. Qiao had them engage in these mock battles at least once and often twice a day. During her first week, Qiao had taken the assignment of fighting Ling herself, which for Ling had been terrifying.

Qiao was the most talented fighter in their Leheqi and the least patient. Thankfully, though, Qiao eventually grew bored with Ling and began assigning her to face off against other children, who each took their turn beating her up.

No matter who she was assigned to fight or how hard she attempted to protect herself, Ling's battles always ended in defeat. When she fought back, her opponents laughed and mocked her by flailing their arms around, trying to mimic the pathetic and awkward way she moved. Any of them, including even the eight-year-old children, could easily defeat her within only a matter of seconds.

In time, Ling learned that her safest course of action was to simply crouch down on the floor and roll up into a ball. This way, the torture would end more quickly. Of course, the other children called her a coward when she did this, but she didn't care. Anything was better than having to go against them directly.

While most of their mocking was done openly, some of their comments were indirect. For Ling, it was these indirect criticisms that hurt her the most. Somehow they felt more valid, probably because the other children presented these comments as factual rather than as intentional insults. Insults could be ignored, but facts were much harder to escape from.

One of the four members of Ling's Xué, named Yue, had an exceptionally well-developed talent for hurting Ling's feelings. She seemed to take great pleasure in pointing out Ling's many failures. Yue was a self-righteous girl who was not particularly talented when it came to fighting but who made up for what she lacked in strength by exhibiting enthusiastic piety.

"Ling, you demonstrate exactly why the Lóng Tiǎozhàn was put into place by our ancestors. The Shī-Dǎoshī is very wise. I think that he wants the rest of us to see and understand what happens when someone unworthy enters into the Nest."

A bit of rice fell out of Yue's mouth as she spoke.

Yue's defining personality trait was how she liked to evangelize the importance of their traditions and the wisdom of the great Dragons who had gone before them. The other two members of her Xué, Qiao and Yanmei, rarely responded to her when she preached like this, but they still treated her with respect and acceptance.

"You are nothing more than a lotus flower who will always be incapable of living up to the ideals of the Lóng Tiǎozhàn. Your example will remind everyone why our ancestors put this test in place. You will bring great dishonor to yourself and your family, but you will save many others who aspire to be more than they are meant to be from following your example. In that way, you will serve the purpose of our wise ShI-Dǎoshī."

Ling didn't respond to Yue. What could she say? Instead, she kept her head down and concentrated on eating her food.

After lunch, Qiao led all sixty-four members of the Blue Engrow Leheqi back upstairs to their training room on the first floor. Once there, she had them practice a series of complicated movements that required the children to balance on one leg while sweeping their foot in a wide arching path over and in front of their heads. They were then supposed to flip around onto their other foot and repeat the same sweeping movement in the opposite direction.

The other children all performed the exercise with relative ease. Even Yue showed few signs of struggle as she moved back and forth between the two stances, first kicking out across 180 degrees, then flipping around to the other side so that she could complete an entire circle with her other leg.

Qiao was so fast that she reminded Ling of a helicopter, while Ling, on the other hand, couldn't even lift her leg above her waist without losing her balance. Nor could she hop from one foot to the other without falling over. So instead of swinging her foot above her head, Ling simply did her best to stick her foot straight out in front of her. She then stopped and, standing on both feet, took multiple steps to turn herself around. Once she was facing the other direction, she then kicked again. By the time she had completed a full rotation, even the slowest of the other children had already gone around five or six times. After just a few minutes, Ling was dizzy and panting from exhaustion, while those around her had barely even begun to break a sweat.

Chapter Fourteen

Though it is true that the great Shā-Shŭ was born in San Francisco, students of history would be wrong to refer to this as his homeland, just as it would be incorrect to refer to the location of a tree by referencing where its seed first originated. The seed may have been blown in from this or that place; however, its home is where it first established its roots. Where it first took in nourishment and matured into a great maple.
—The Book of the Wyvern Spirits

For the second night in a row, Apollo didn't sleep well. He kept having nightmares of Ai-An performing various duties. Some of which were so strange that he would have laughed at their absurdity if Apollo had been awake. After completing one of these duties, she would then look over at him and say, "I'm sorry, Shā-Shŭ. I am only doing my duty." Apollo would then look down at himself in these dreams and discover that he was no longer a boy and Instead had become a gerbil. In contrast, Ai-An had transformed herself into a powerful dragon.

Exhausted, he eventually gave up on sleeping and instead rolled over onto his back so that he could watch the dim light in his window begin to brighten. Then, when the sunlight indicated that it was almost time for breakfast, he sat up on his and leaned against the wall. So that when Shīfù Hui arrived, Apollo was waiting for him with his legs crossed and arms folded.

It was the first time Apollo had been awake and sitting up when Shīfù Hui came into the room to collect him in the morning. His teacher first glanced toward Apollo and then at his pillow, where his book still lay. Though he didn't say anything, Apollo could tell that Shīfù Hui was pleased. After a brief pause, the man turned and gestured for Apollo to follow him to breakfast.

Just as had happened during the previous few days, Apollo once again felt Ai-An watching him as he walked across the dining room. He knew that all she wanted was to see some sign that he didn't hate her.

Apollo was beginning to feel ashamed of himself for being so cruel. Ai-An was the only child in the school who was nice to him. Eventually, he would have to forgive her. It wasn't as though he had many other options for making friends here. He needed her. For now, though, he still wanted her to suffer. She deserved to feel bad for thinking that it was her duty to allow him to be humiliated.

After breakfast, Apollo followed Shīfù Hui back to his room. Once alone, he again set himself to the task of trying to study the blue book. Instead of just skimming through a few pages at random, as he had done up until then, he decided that he would examine each page individually, starting from the beginning.

He did his best, but after only a few pages, Apollo's eyes grew heavy, and his mind began to wander. He became frustrated and once again started to question the logic of the assignment that Shīfù Hui had given him. It was tedious, and Apollo was pretty sure the only thing he was getting out of the exercise was a headache.

Irritable and sleepy, Apollo decided that he would take a short, five-minute nap, after which he figured he could continue again with a fresh mind. Apollo took Ling's coin out from underneath his mat and used it as a bookmark, placing the coin in the crease between the two pages where he had left off. He then shut the book and laid it across his chest. Leaning his head back onto his pillow, Apollo closed his eyes. Soon, the book began to rise and fall with his breathing.

Several hours must have passed when he was unexpectedly awoken by the familiar kick of his teacher, who had come into his room to collect him for lunch.

The blue book still lay on his chest, which evidently impressed Shīfù Hui because he nodded approvingly.

After lunch, Apollo again sat down on his mat and continued flipping through the book's pages. He wasn't nearly as tired as he had been in the morning. However, the chore was still excruciatingly dull.

As his fingers absentmindedly flipped over the pages, Apollo's attention wandered. He once again began to think about dragons and how Shīfù Hui had instructed him that the feet of a dragon carried the mythical creatures toward their duty. Apollo tried to imagine how a gerbil's tiny feet might be useful.

These thoughts reminded him of when he had seen gerbils in a local pet store back in San Francisco. In the middle of the store, there had been several large open-air cages filled with various animals. A sign posted on the wall above the pens read that it was okay for store visitors to pet and touch the rodents. The cage containing gerbils was filled with little fluffy balls which were all quietly sleeping.

Apollo had undoubtedly done a lot of sleeping lately, but he didn't think it was a very ennobling trait. If that was all gerbils did, they probably weren't very admirable.

Then again, it really wasn't fair to judge the little animals based on a single experience. Gerbils must have had other qualities besides just the ability to sleep. Anyway, weren't they nocturnal? He had only ever watched them that single time, during the day.

Gerbils certainly didn't roar like dragons, but if a gerbil wanted to, it could probably chirp loudly enough to be heard. Apollo was pretty sure that if he held a gerbil too tightly, it would bite. The more he tried, the easier it became for Apollo to come up with other positive traits exhibited by these little animals.

For example, Apollo supposed that gerbils would probably stand their ground just as ferociously as any dragon when it came to protecting what was important to them, like their young.

Apollo remembered what his mother had once said about being strong. It occurred to him that if any animal could be considered both quiet and unassuming, while also having hidden strength, that a gerbil certainly could. These little animals might not be loud or say much, but they did know what was important to them.

Everyone admired the dragons. But wasn't it more often the gerbils who ran around underfoot, quietly advancing the goals of humanity. They might not always be noticed like the dragons were, but gerbils knew who they were. They knew what they stood for and when to hold their ground.

A few days earlier, Shīfù Hui had advised Apollo that he could choose to follow the footsteps of a dragon. However, Apollo now wondered why he couldn't just remain a gerbil. Or perhaps he could be both a dragon and a gerbil at the same time.

Perhaps he could honor Shīfù Hui's teachings and strive to do his duty, walking in the footsteps of a dragon or whatever it was that his teacher wanted him to do, while at the same time also remaining true to his mother's definition of strength.

Apollo stretched and yawned. He had now flipped through almost half of the blue book and decided that it was time to take another break.

Apollo took out Ling's coin and once again placed it into the crease between the two pages he had just finished scanning. He then sat the book down and looked up at the window. It was getting dark, which meant that Shīfù Hui would be coming in to get him for dinner soon.

Apollo stood up, stretched a second time, and decided to spend the rest of the evening practicing gymnastics. It had been days since he had done anything physical. It would feel good to be active again.

During dinner, Apollo finally looked at Ai-An. His determination to remain angry at her had gradually been replaced by a desire to understand her better. He was beginning to see her in a new light. She hadn't grown up with a mom like Tayleigh Salvatoir. If she had, then perhaps like him, she too would have learned to be loyal to her friends. Instead, Ai-An had grown up with teachers like Shīfù Hui, who spoke of dragon's feet and loyalty to duty. Though he wanted to remain upset with her, Apollo found it difficult and unfair to blame Ai-An for being true to her upbringing.

As he looked into her eyes, her expression pleaded for his forgiveness. Apollo smiled, and she immediately smiled back, relief rushing across her face. Ai-An closed her eyes for a moment and then dabbed at them with a cloth napkin. She looked up at Apollo again and nodded softly while taking in a deep breath. Apollo couldn't help himself. He forgave her completely. If she cared that much about their friendship, then he couldn't feel anything other than gratitude toward her.

Apollo felt an unexpected rush of confidence. Before he knew what he was doing, he stood up and started walking directly toward Ai-An. He wasn't sure what he was going to do until he got there. When Apollo reached the table where Ai-An was seated, he turned toward Lei.

He then did the most difficult thing that he had ever done up to that point in his entire life. Apollo looked into Lei's eyes and bowed his head toward him. Showing him the same respect that the other children did. Apollo then returned to his place against the wall without saying a word and sat back down.

After a moment, he looked up at Ai-An. She was now fully and unabashedly smiling at him, no longer trying to hide it or to be subtle. Lei was also looking at him. Apollo was surprised to see Lei nod slightly toward him in approval.

Apollo was dumbfounded. The boy who had been his enemy was now, through a single act of submission, bound to him through duty. Apollo knew that he and Lei were not friends, but they were also no longer enemies.

Apollo looked over at the table where the adults were seated. Shīfù Hui was also looking at Apollo, and like Ai-An, he, too, was radiating pride.

After the other students left the dining room, Shīfù Hui walked over to where Apollo was waiting for him.

"You have found your feet, Apollo. You have performed your duty."

Apollo bowed. "Shīfù Hui, I would like you to call me Shā-Shŭ."

Apollo had been grateful to Shīfù Hui for using his real name. It had meant a lot to him when *Shā-Shŭ* had felt like an insult. Now, though, he was beginning to identify with the name just as much as he did with the name Apollo. It reminded him of his mother and the boy she wanted him to become. Using the name Shā-Shŭ would help keep Apollo grounded in her expectations for him.

Shīfù Hui smiled and nodded.

"Shā-Shŭ, you have brought yourself great honor tonight. You may return to your room without my assistance."

With that, Shīfù Hui turned and left Apollo standing alone in the dining room. Apollo moved quickly and with deliberate purpose. It was a very small thing to be allowed to walk to his room alone, but he was going to make sure that he did it right this time. Shīfù Hui trusted him, and he wasn't going to let him down.

Apollo was now more determined than ever to follow his teacher's instructions. Each morning he woke up before his teacher arrived. When Shīfù Hui came into the room to collect him, he was usually already sitting on his mat. After meals, Apollo was then allowed to return to his room unattended.

On the third day of this new routine, while once again absentmindedly flipping through the pages of his book, Apollo found something that he hadn't noticed before. Folded up and tucked into the pages about three-fourths of the way toward the back of the book, there was a loose piece of paper.

Apollo removed it and then unfolded the paper, where he discovered a painting that immediately impressed him. The thin, almost silk-like page contained a delicately drawn dragon. Apollo traced the blue feet of the dragon with his finger and from there ran his hand up toward the wings, which were bright orange. He placed the image on the floor and used his hands to smooth it out. The dragon had four green heads and powerful-looking arms. It looked like it was about to attack using a single, very sharp-looking claw, which it held out in front of itself.

Apollo knelt above the painting and squinted in an attempt to see it better. Half of the dragon was covered in intricately drawn scales, which ran from the tip of two of his heads down its back. The other two heads seemed to have smooth, unprotected skin.

Two white flames extended from one of its mouths, which fanned outward in opposite directions. A third flame shot out of another mouth while the remaining two heads bore their fangs. The picture was so vivid that Apollo could almost hear the dragon growling.

There was writing next to the dragon's feet, wings, and each of its four heads, which Apollo couldn't read. The writing that interested Apollo the most, though, were dark characters that appeared in the upper-right corner of the painting, which Apollo assumed must have been the title.

He recognized them immediately. They were probably the only Chinese symbols that Apollo was familiar with. He had no idea what they meant, but he had seen them before. They were the same characters that appeared on the back of the coin Ling had given him. Ling's coin was one of the only possessions he still had that actually belonged to him. He had spent many hours playing with and examining it. Every millimeter of that coin was familiar to him.

Apollo leaned back on his mat and stretched out his legs.

Why were the same symbols that appeared on Ling's coin also on a painting he had found inside Shīfù Huì's book? Not just one of these characters, but all of them, and in the same order. Perhaps the characters spelled out some famous Chinese saying, like how the phrase *In God We Trust* appears both on American money and some American art.

Apollo carefully checked again. He hadn't imagined it. Every character on the coin perfectly matched those written across the top of the painting. He set the coin down so that he could refold the picture. Apollo then placed both the image and Ling's coin back into the center of his book.

He then stood up and ran his fingers through his hair. He felt frustrated by how little he actually understood about this place. He had spent several months here but hadn't learned anything about where he was or why he had been sent there.

In California, the other students his age were undoubtedly progressing through the sixth grade. They were learning about science, math, history, and English, while he had spent the entire school year in the basement of an old building on the other side of the world. Where the only thing he had learned was how to sit quietly against the wall, and something he even didn't understand about dragon feet.

Chapter Fifteen

It has been suggested by a few less informed writers that Jiàn Hui's childhood was one of disobedience and indulgence and that without the influence of the great Shā-Shǔ, he would have remained a lost and fallen soul. Though these writers deserve our respect, their conclusions seem altogether unlikely. We know from the writings of many, including those of the Shā-Shǔ himself, that the Shā-Shǔ greatly reverenced his teacher. So much so that he credited him as having been the most significant influence in his life. How then can we suppose that this man who was so revered by the Shā-Shǔ could have lived anything less than a life of honor and nobility? It seems that any notion to the contrary must be resoundingly rejected.
—The Book of the Wyvern Spirits

Since the birth of his son and the subsequent death of his dear wife, Biyu, Jiàn Hui had felt nothing other than heartbreak and remorse. Biyu had lived just long enough to hold their son in her arms and kiss him on the forehead.

For a few brief moments, everything in his life had seemed perfect. His beautiful wife and his handsome new son were together with him. He should have thanked the Wyvern Spirits right then and there for the blessing of such a miracle. But he didn't. Instead, he congratulated himself for the accomplishment of having selected such a pretty wife and for having created that little boy with her. He took all of the credit and gave them none.

It was only a few moments after these boastful thoughts had passed through his mind that the Wyvern Spirits inflicted their punishment on him. Biyu's face turned purple, and she began to gasp for air. The Yīshēng later told him that it was a blood clot that had formed during their son's birth that had killed Biyu. But Hui knew the truth. A blood clot might have been the tool the Wyvern Spirits used, but it wasn't the cause. The cause had been his own disobedience. This was a punishment that was being placed on him for a lifetime of misdeeds.

Not just for the ingratitude that he had expressed during a single moment of pride. The Wyvern Spirits were, after all, fair and patient. If this single transgression had been his only offense, he was confident it would have been overlooked. Unfortunately for his family, though, his expression of arrogance had been just the latest in a lifetime of similar acts. He had tempted the patience of the Wyvern Spirits too many times.

At last, they had decided that he was no longer worthy of propagating the family name. They had waited until he was most vulnerable. Then they struck at him in a way that was so profoundly painful to make it impossible for Hui to ignore them.

Had he followed the example of his older brother, Aiguo, his wife and son would have been protected. Unlike his brother, though, Hui had never really committed himself to the Dragon's Dance. As a child, he always viewed Aiguo's commitment to the Order as excessive, even extreme. During the sixteen years that he spent training in the Yuándīng Temple, Aiguo had been well-liked and widely admired, not just by the other children but also by the adults.

Even their father had preferred Aiguo over Hui. He had been so proud of his older son and disappointed in the younger one. The two brothers were very different right from their births, the older brother remaining true to his father's expectations, while the younger showed more interest in experiencing the pleasures of life than in performing his duties.

At eight years old, on his first day in the Yuándīng Temple, Aiguo was awarded the title of Qiān-lóng of his entire Leheqi. Of course, leading the three other members of your own Xué was a tremendous honor and accomplishment any parent would have been proud of. But to be put in charge of all sixty-four members of the Blue Engrow Leheqi on his very first day of training was almost unheard of.

His father bragged to anyone who would listen to him about how most children who served as Qiān-lóng only achieved the rank during their fourth and final year in a Leheqi, whereas his son had managed to do it on his very first day. At the age of only eight, he would be leading children much older than himself.

Not only had Aiguo been named to the position on his first day, but from that time forward, he never lost his title. During his entire time training as a Blue Engrow, an Orange Poppy, a Green Dahlia, and a White Lily, Aiguo had remained the unquestioned leader of each of these Leheqis.

Not surprisingly, this brought him the admiration of the entire village. When people spoke of the Jiàn family, it was Aiguo whose name they revered. In the eyes of the people, Hui was nothing more than Aiguo's little brother.

The year that Hui himself turned eight, there had been forty-six other children in the village who also reached the age of the Lóng Tiǎozhàn. Under tremendous pressure from his father, Aiguo spent countless hours preparing Hui at home so that he would be ready. With the help of his brother, Hui was successful in passing the tests, earning himself a dragon tattoo just like that of Aiguo, while also claiming his place as one of the sixteen children who would grow up and train in the Dragon's Nest. His position as one of the most elite members of the village was from that point on forever sealed.

A lifetime of obedience, honor, and duty now stretched out in front of Hui, all before he was old enough to understand the many sacrifices that it would require him to make. He didn't resent his father or brother, though, for having pushed him down this path, mostly because he soon realized that Dragons enjoyed certain advantages in the community. The biggest of these was the admiration of the village girls, many of whom hoped to tie their fortunes to his. Hui soon discovered that he could enjoy these benefits while only half-heartedly committing himself to the sacrifices.

The adults who administered the Temple affairs weren't used to disobedience. As such, they were very trusting, which made it easy for Hui and some of his friends to sneak out, something they frequently did so that they could spend their nights drinking baijiu in the company of various village girls.

Throughout his training in the Temple, Aiguo became the center of attention for those committed to the Dragon's Creed. In contrast, Hui became the center of activity for those who would rather spend their time enjoying the experiences life had to offer.

Now, many years later, Aiguo led one of the Dǎoshī's most trusted Xué and was on a path that would bring him great honor. Most of the villagers expected him to take the place of Shi Ju-Long as the Dǎoshī when their current leader's time came to an end. As the leader of the Yuándīng Temple and ruler over the village of Daletezhen, Aiguo would then be remembered by their people forever. A hundred generations from now, his name would still be recorded in the Lotus Room scrolls as one who had served as Dǎoshī.

While Hui was destined to disappear into obscurity and to be forgotten by even his own family, which was the message that the Wyvern Spirits had so cruelly sent to him on the night of Biyu's death. Now that it was too late, he bitterly wished that he could undo his past mistakes.

On the day she had died, Hui went out behind his home, wrapped himself in their family's Dragon Cloak, and cried out to the Wyvern Spirits in his garden. His neighbors could hear him, but he didn't care. He called out to the sky, pleading for forgiveness and for them to restore his little family to him.

In their great mercy, the Wyvern Spirits showed Hui compassion. As he prayed to them, they whispered their penance into his heart. They reminded Hui that they had allowed his son to live. Hui realized that he could still have a second chance through this little boy. The Wyvern Spirits had granted him the opportunity to raise his son to be a better man than he had been.

That night Hui stood up in his garden, and in the presence of the innumerable unseen Wyvern Spirits, he committed himself to this task with full purpose of heart. He promised that he would teach his son to understand the importance of performing the Dragon's Dance and ensure that he was well-versed in the Dragon's Creed.

In time, Hui eventually began to find some measure of joy in his life again. When his son turned eight years old, he passed the Lóng Tiǎozhàn and entered into the Yuándīng Temple as a Dragon. Like his uncle Aiguo, Hui's son was also made Qiān-lóng of his Leheqi during his first year, something that hadn't happened in a generation, not since Aiguo himself had done it. As a result, Hui's son now stood at the center of honor, restoring the family's name.

In the end, though, his little boy turned out to be too much like his father. While outwardly performing his duties with tremendous honor, he inwardly harbored the same rebellious spirit Hui himself had exhibited in his youth.

Guided by this defiance, his son left the Temple alone one night, probably to explore the countryside or escape some of the pressures of his training. While walking outside the safety of the village, he fell off a ridge in the neighboring ravine.

In the year that followed the death of his son, Jiàn Hui descended into a deep depression.

Nothing he had ever experienced in his life could have prepared him for the agony and grief he felt over the loss of his son. His pain was profoundly dark. He had loved his wife, but Hui had invested so much more into his precious little boy.

Hui retreated into his home, where he ignored his duty to his Xué and spent the next several months lying on the floor in his front room, willing himself to die. What purpose was there in prolonging his miserable life?

When the Dǎoshī came to his home to visit him, Hui expected to be chastised for retreating from his duties. Instead of disciplining him, though, the Dǎoshī spoke to Hui about what he referred to as a sacred commission. Something about an American boy coming to stay with them at the Yuándīng Temple.

The Dǎoshī stressed the importance of the assignment. No American had ever visited the village before, let alone entered their Temple. Outsiders were not allowed. It was absolutely forbidden. But the Dǎoshī told Hui that bringing the American here was an order from the ShI-Dǎoshī himself. Hui was to monitor the boy, keep him alive, and make sure that he stayed in the basement, keeping him away from the rest of the Temple.

At first, Jiàn Hui felt honored to have been selected for such an important assignment. However, it didn't take him long to realize that watching the boy was, in the end, just a clever way for the Dǎoshī to punish him.

On the night of the annual Lóng Tiǎozhàn, as the entire village gathered into the Temple dressed in their finest clothing, Apollo showed up looking like a mud rat. To make matters worse, when Hui had ordered the boy to wait outside, the child had acted with insubordination and arrogance.

Despite how the boy presented himself, though, Hui still performed his duty. After helping the other adults orient the new Dragon nestlings into the Temple, Hui brought the boy to the basement as he had been instructed to do and provided him with a place to sleep.

Beyond this, Hui didn't care what happened to Apollo. If it hadn't been for Ai An, he wouldn't have even allowed the boy the luxury of clean clothes or a bathing sponge.

Ai-An reminded Hui of his wife. She was sweet, thoughtful, and always seemed to put others ahead of herself. But, more importantly, she had belonged to the same Xué as his son. Though his son was now a Wyvern Spirit, Hui still felt loyal to them. So when Ai-An asked for permission to bring the American boy clean clothes and a bathing sponge each night, Hui couldn't find it within himself to tell her no, even though initially he didn't think the boy deserved such luxuries.

Lately, though, Hui's feelings for the boy had begun to change. In the months since Apollo's arrival, Hui found himself beginning to grow more fond of him. While Apollo knew nothing of the Dragon's Dance and was completely undisciplined, he exhibited some of the same traits that Hui's own precious son had shown. Or perhaps Hui only imagined these traits in the boy. Maybe he was just desperate to feel some sort of a connection to his son again.

Regardless, Hui repeatedly saw little flashes of courage in the boy that betrayed his true character. Hui found himself wondering what kind of Dragon Apollo might have become had he grown up here in the village instead of in some barbaric American city.

Shi Ju-Long had made it clear that Apollo was to be told nothing about why he was there or about the work that went on upstairs. Hui's job was only to keep the boy alive until the time when the ShI-Dǎoshī was ready to take him away again.

However, despite these strict orders, Jiàn Hui's curiosity got the better of him. In the end, he decided to leave it up to the Wyvern Spirits. He would give the boy an impossible challenge. If Apollo was successful, he would know that the Wyvern Spirits wanted the boy to be trained. Hui didn't dare go against a direct order from his Dǎoshī. However, he realized that the Dǎoshī's instructions had left him an opportunity. Shi Ju-Long had only told him that he couldn't teach the boy. He didn't say anything about allowing Apollo to learn on his own.

Jiàn Hui returned to his home and retrieved his copy of the sacred *Way of the Dragon*. It was the same book his father had once given to him and that his son had carried during his time in the Temple. He was about to return to the Temple when a picture his mother had once painted caught his eye. Did the Wyvern Spirits also want Hui to give this picture to the American boy? Unsure, he took it down from the wall. Removed it from its frame and carefully folded it. He then gently tucked the silky paper into one of the pages of the book. If the Wyvern Spirits wanted the boy to have it, they would lead him to find it.

Hui knew that his challenge for Apollo was unfair. Apollo couldn't read Chinese, which was what made the test so perfect. Hui figured that if the Wyvern Spirits really did want Apollo to learn the Dragon's Dance, then they would perform a miracle and open up the boy's mind to the book's knowledge. If they didn't, then his mind would remain shut, in which case, there would be no harm in Hui having given him the opportunity.

Chapter Sixteen

We must remember that during the Shā-Shǔ's childhood, San Francisco had not yet joined the Great Awakening. Yet despite this, the Shā-Shǔ still managed to somehow master the Dragon's Dance and perform it flawlessly during his first attempt. What can be said of such a feat? How could a young boy who had no prior knowledge of the Lóng Tiǎozhàn attain the skills necessary to succeed? Let us not forget that this is something that takes most children years to prepare for. It certainly would not be an exaggeration to call his performance that day miraculous.
—*The Book of the Wyvern Spirits*

Apollo passed Ai-An in the hall one evening on his way back to his room after dinner. When she noticed him walking toward her, she picked up her pace and then self-consciously grabbed her arm with her free hand. In her other hand, she was holding a small sack. Apollo didn't ask or even care what was inside the little bundle. He was more interested in taking advantage of the fact that they were alone together, an opportunity they had never had before.

There were a million things he wanted to say to her. Questions that he wanted to ask. Rather than greeting her, he instead requested Ai-An to wait for him, telling her that he would be right back. She looked at him curiously and was about to say something, but before she could respond, Apollo ran off toward his room, which was only a few doors away. Once there, he grabbed the dragon painting hidden inside his book and then quickly made his way back to where Ai-An was standing.

Ai-An looked genuinely surprised and also a bit uneasy to see Apollo holding the picture.

"Shā-Shǔ, how did you get that?"

"Shīfù Hui gave it to me. He told me that I was supposed to study it."

Apollo left out the part about how Shīfù Hui hadn't actually given him the painting directly but had instead given him a blue book and that he had found the dragon picture inside the book.

Telling Ai-An that the picture had been given to him by Shīfù Hui seemed to put her more at ease. This was good because Apollo intended to get as much information out of her as possible.

"What does this say?" Apollo pointed toward the title at the top.

"It says 'The Dance of the Dragons.'" Ai-An looked at Apollo, shaking her head doubtfully. "I thought you said Shīfù Hui gave it to you?"

"He did. He just didn't tell me anything about it."

Apollo looked at the image and tried to imagine the four-headed dragon dancing.

"What is the dance of the dragons?" he asked.

Ai-An shook her head and giggled in a way that suggested the answer was incredibly obvious. Apollo didn't like her laughing at him. It made him feel foolish.

"The Dance of the Dragons is everything, Shā-Shǔ," she teased, raising one of her eyebrows.

"Ai-An, I don't understand. What do you mean it's everything?"

"You really don't know anything about the Dragon's Dance?" Ai-An looked up from the painting and then directly into Apollo's eyes. "Did Jian Hui really give this to you?"

"Yes." Apollo sounded a bit more irritated than he meant to. He took a deep breath to calm himself.

"I'm sorry, Ai-An, it's just frustrating to be kept down here and not know anything. Shīfù Hui told me to study everything I could about the Dance of the Dragons."

He didn't like telling Ai-An half-truths. Shīfù Hui hadn't exactly told him to study the dance of the dragons, or whatever it was that she had called it. But he did tell Apollo that the blue book contained everything Apollo needed to be successful and that he should study it carefully. The only thing inside that book that he could even remotely understand was this painting, which according to Ai-An, had something to do with dancing dragons.

"What does this say?" Apollo pointed to the characters by the dragon's feet.

"It's the first part of the Dragon's Creed. It says, 'The feet of a dragon stand firm against evil, walking toward and never away from duty.'"

"What is the dragon's creed?"

"Shā-Shǔ, I have to get back to my Xué. I was only supposed to be gone for a few minutes. They're going to come looking for me."

The seriousness in Ai-An's expression made it clear to him that she wasn't exaggerating. Apollo knew she was never separated from Fānyì and Lei, except for a few minutes each evening during dinner. However, he also knew she was evading his question.

He wanted to insist that she answer him, but this was their first real conversation together, and he didn't want to upset her.

More importantly, Apollo worried what would happen if Lei found him holding the dragon painting. Ai-An's reaction to seeing him with it made Apollo less confident about showing the picture to anyone else. He decided it would be safer not to take any chances.

He nodded and quickly folded the painting back up so he could hide it in his hand. He then walked with Ai-An back down the hallway toward the stairs.

"I am glad, Shā-Shǔ, that you are learning your duty." Ai-An smiled and brushed a loose strand of hair away from her eyes as she turned toward the staircase.

"I am glad that you are helping me." Apollo waved awkwardly.

Ai-An returned his wave and then began walking up the stairs. Apollo watched her until she reached the point where the stairs curved away, bringing her out of his view.

His brief conversation with Ai-An, while not very long, had still been helpful. She hadn't told him very much, but he had learned a few things.

When his teacher arrived in his room to collect him for breakfast the following day, Apollo remained seated on his mat, with his back against the wall. He bowed his head to Shīfù Hui and then, still looking down, asked him about what Ai-An had told him.

"Shīfù, what is the Dragon's Creed?"

164

Apollo didn't look up. He didn't want to allow Shīfù Hui to gesture for him to stand. Apollo hoped that his teacher would feel obligated to reply as long as he kept his head down.

Apollo heard the man moving and, for a moment, worried that he was just going to leave the room. To Apollo's relief, though, Shīfù Hui sat down on the floor in front of him. His teacher's eyes were uncharacteristically emotional. After a few moments, he began to speak.

"The Dragon's Creed is what we all must live by, Shā-Shǔ. It governs our actions and teaches us right from wrong."

Apollo glanced toward the ceiling as he did his best to recite the phrase Shīfù Hui had spoken to him several weeks earlier. "The feet of a dragon stand firm against evil, walking toward and never away from duty?"

"That is part of the Dragon's Creed, yes. But there is much more."

"What is the rest?"

Shīfù Hui examined Apollo thoughtfully. Apparently trying to decide how much he should say. After a moment, he began to speak again.

"We learn the Dragon's Creed only when we are ready to live up to its teachings."

Apollo was unwilling to accept his teacher's answer. Not when he was finally so close to understanding something important about this place.

"Please, Shīfù Hui. I don't understand."

"And that, Shā-Shǔ, is why you are not yet ready to learn the rest of the creed."

"How am I supposed to be ready if no one will help me prepare?"

Shīfù Hui paused, considering Apollo for a moment. Then, speaking more to himself than Apollo, he muttered under his breath, "You did follow your duty when you bowed to the Qiān-lóng of the Blue Engrow Leheqi."

Apollo responded hopefully. "I want to follow all of my duties, Shīfù. I just need someone to tell me what they are."

Shīfù Hui hesitated, looking both simultaneously impressed while also uncertain. "I guess there wouldn't be any harm in helping you. But Shā-Shŭ, you must promise me that you will follow the second precept of the Creed just as faithfully as you have followed the first."

"I will do my best. I promise." Apollo tried not to sound too eager.

Seemingly satisfied, Shīfù Hui pointed toward Apollo's arms. "The wings of a dragon carry them to those who are in need of help."

"I don't have wings." Apollo blurted out stupidly.

"No, that is true. You don't have wings."

Recovering himself, Apollo asked, "Then how can I follow the second part of the Creed?"

"That is something that you must work out for yourself." Shīfù Hui stood and straightened out his robes. "Now, let's go, or we will be late for breakfast."

He left Apollo and began to walk down the passageway. Apollo hurried to catch up to him. Reaching his teacher just a few feet outside his door.

"What about the Dragon's Dance?"

Shīfù Hui stopped walking and looked directly into Apollo's eyes. "How do you know about the Dragon's Dance?" he asked.

Apollo swallowed hard, searching his mind for how to answer him. He didn't want to get Ai-An in trouble. "It was, um, in the book that you gave me," he lied.

Shīfù Hui looked at Apollo carefully and then started walking again. Speaking in a much softer voice than before, "Shā-Shǔ, it is best that we do not talk about the Dragon's Dance. Especially not while we are outside your room."

Chapter Seventeen

Do we revere the great Shā-Shǔ because he united all of us around a common set of ideals? Do we honor him because of his teachings of compassion and gentleness? Do we admire him for being the youngest ShI-Dǎoshī ever to hold the office? Do we respect him because of his skill in battle? The answer to all of these questions is a resounding Yes. Before the Shā-Shǔ found his destiny, the world was a very different place than it is today. He changed it more profoundly than almost any other individual who has ever lived.

—The Book of the Wyvern Spirits

For as long as Apollo could remember, he had always admired his dad. To him, his father had been a larger-than-life figure. This was why Apollo had been willing to forgive him for never having had the time to take him to baseball games or on hikes. He knew that his dad held the weight of a large business empire on his shoulders, and that was something Apollo had always felt that he could be proud of.

Lately, though, Apollo was beginning to doubt his father's character. Ever since arriving here at the school, Apollo found himself with a lot of time on his hands to think. On top of that, his daily interactions with Shīfù Hui gave him a new perspective. His teacher was the only other male role model Apollo had ever really spent significant time with.

Apollo's doubts about his father came into focus when he realized something that surprised him. One morning, while walking to breakfast with Shīfù Hui, it occurred to Apollo that he had spoken to his teacher over the past few months more than he had spoken to his father throughout his entire life. Which, considering how little Shīfù Hui spoke, was significant.

During most of his time at the school, his interactions with Shīfù Hui had been cold and unaffectionate. However, the more time they spent together, the better Apollo read his moods. Periodically, the man had shown Apollo kindness, and occasionally something more. Not love, precisely, but a similar type of emotion. Shīfù Hui cared for Apollo, or at least Apollo was pretty sure he did. He certainly cared whether or not Apollo advanced in his studies.

Taking an interest in his life was something his father had never done. Now that he was experiencing it from Shīfù Hui, Apollo was beginning to realize how starved for this type of attention he had always been.

Growing up, Apollo made excuses for his father's lack of involvement in his life. Now, these excuses were beginning to feel empty, leaving behind the dull realization that his dad's businesses mattered more to him than his own son did.

Apollo had always blamed himself and his awkwardness for his dad's lack of interest in him. Why would a man like William Salvatoir, who everyone admired and who had the command of any room he entered into, want anything to do with a boy who never knew what to say and who couldn't do anything right?

He would have continued blaming himself, too, if it hadn't been for the attentions of Shīfù Hui. If a man who wasn't even his relative could take such an interest in him, then it shouldn't be too much to ask for his own father to speak to him occasionally or to come to one of his gymnastics competitions.

The more time he spent under the care of Shīfù Hui, the more crucial his teacher's opinion became to him. Apollo didn't want to disappoint the man. If Shīfù Hui wanted Apollo to learn to follow the Dragon's Creed, then doing this was also important to Apollo. In an effort to do this, he frequently reviewed the first two precepts of the Creed in his mind.

The feet of a dragon stand firm against evil, walking toward and never away from duty…

The wings of a dragon carry them to those who are in need of help…

According to Shīfù Hui, Apollo had already proven himself when it came to the first precept by crossing the dining room and bowing to Lei. Since then, he had continued following his duty by strictly obeying the rules Shīfù Hui gave him, including spending at least part of each day flipping through the pages of his book and always making sure to return directly to his room after meals.

Apollo knew that if he wanted to continue learning the rest of the creed, then he would first have to find a way to show Shīfù Hui that he was willing to live the second precept. Knowing that this was what he had to do was much easier, though, than doing it. How could he use his wings to fly to those who required his help when he was stuck in a basement?

The only people he encountered down there were all so much stronger than he was. None of them needed anything that he could offer them, and he wasn't permitted to leave his prison to look for opportunities to help others anywhere else. Whatever he did would have to be accomplished within the boundaries of this dungeon.

During dinner one evening, an idea occurred to Apollo that he couldn't believe he had overlooked. The children and teachers weren't the only people in the basement. He had completely forgotten about the old woman who prepared all their meals and cleaned up after them.

As far as Apollo knew, she did her work alone. He had never seen anyone else working with her. He assumed that preparing three large meals each day and cleaning up after everyone couldn't be an easy job. Especially not for someone as old as she appeared to be.

Apollo decided to see if she would let him work with her. He waited until after dinner, allowing everyone else to leave the dining room. When the space was empty, Apollo stood up and walked toward the nearest table, where he began stacking up plates and gathering used chopsticks and napkins together.

By the time the old woman entered the dining room, Apollo was already working on his fifth table. He kept his head down and continued stacking plates, worried that she might get angry with him or tell him to stop and send him back to his room. But, instead, she just looked at him, shook her head in amusement, and then joined in alongside him. When they finished clearing all the tables, the woman allowed Apollo to wash and dry the dishes.

The two worked together in silence for about an hour, after which Apollo returned to his room and went to bed. The following morning after breakfast, he repeated the same gesture, this time feeling much more comfortable and at ease.

He didn't have to worry now that he might upset the woman. It was also easier because he had a better sense of how to complete the chores that needed to be done. During the previous evening, Apollo and the woman had worked out an unspoken routine between them. Now all he had to do was complete the same tasks.

Apollo once again collected the dishes, chopsticks, and napkins, which he carried into the kitchen through a small door behind the food table. He placed the dirty napkins in a basket near the back of the kitchen and then started washing the dishes and chopsticks. He put the clean dishes on a wooden shelf at the side of the room and the chopsticks in a small box sitting on one of the tables. When he was done, Apollo once again bowed his head to the old woman and returned to his room.

By the end of the second day, Apollo felt rather pleased with himself. This had been the most enjoyable day he had experienced at the school. Having something to do for someone else gave Apollo an increased sense of pride and greater confidence in himself.

On the fourth day, when Shīfù Hui came into his room to collect Apollo for lunch, his teacher looked at him sternly and asked, "Shā-Shǔ, why do you help Lanfen clean up the tables?"

"You know I do that?" Apollo had wanted Shīfù Hui to notice him. Getting seen by his teacher was the point of helping the old woman. However, Apollo hadn't yet found the courage to start helping her before his teacher left the dining room. Apollo wasn't aware that Shīfù Hui had ever observed his efforts. Apparently, though, he had.

"Of course, I know. You are my responsibility. You are my only responsibility."

Shīfù Hui leaned down so that his face was now only a foot or so away from Apollo's before continuing.

"What I don't understand are your motives for being disobedient. It is her duty to clean up the tables. It is your duty to return to your room directly after each meal."

Apollo swallowed and looked down at his feet, doing his best to search for any words that might justify his actions.

"Shīfù, you told me that the wings of a dragon must carry them to help those who are in need. The woman who cleans the dining room needed help. I—" Apollo looked down at his feet again and lowered his voice. "I just thought I could help her."

"Shā-Shǔ, it is good that you are trying to help others. But obedience to your duties comes before helping those in need. A dragon cannot stand without his feet. Remember, first, the feet of a dragon stand firm against evil, walking toward and never away from duty. Only then can the wings of a dragon carry him to those who are in need of his help. Without his feet, a dragon will stumble and fall."

"Yes, Shīfù." Apollo again lowered his head. "May I have permission to help the woman clean up after meals?" Again, Apollo kept his head down while waiting for Shīfù Hui's answer.

"Yes, my Shā-Shǔ. Use your wings and fly to Lanfen in the kitchen. But afterward, you must still return directly to your room."

Shīfù Hui reached out and took Apollo by the face, lifting his head so that they were again looking eye to eye. "Shā-Shǔ, it is essential that you remain true to your word. From now on, you must always fulfill your duty. Promise me that you will never disobey me again."

Apollo closed his eyes and nodded. "Yes, Shīfù, I promise. Thank you."

Shīfù Hui let go of Apollo's face, but he didn't immediately leave the room. Instead, after a few moments, he spoke again.

"I think that you are ready for the third precept. The head of a dragon must seek learning and knowledge throughout its entire life."

With that, Shīfù Hui turned and left Apollo's room, gesturing for him to follow.

Chapter Eighteen

We are no less astonished now in adulthood as when we were children to read of the exploits of the great Shā-Shǔ. We are no less thrilled now than we were then to see his sagas acted out in plays or spoken of in poetic verse. We sing the nursery rhyme 'The Little Dragon Boy' with the same eagerness of spirit as does the four-year-old child sitting on the floor clapping to the music. The legend that he left in his wake will undoubtedly continue to inspire people for thousands of years.
—The Book of the Wyvern Spirits

Two days earlier, when Apollo had given his word to obey his teacher, he had been completely sincere. However, during the few days that had passed since then, he already found himself planning to break his vow.

He knew that if he got caught, he would be disciplined, which, of course, was something he wanted to avoid. But, what concerned him even more, was how his actions might disappoint his teacher.

He justified this disobedience by telling himself that his plan would allow him to follow the rest of Shīfù Hui's teachings more faithfully. Rather than admitting to himself his much more selfish motive, which was that he wanted to satisfy his own curiosity.

Apollo was tired of always being in the dark and feeling lost. He was tired of being left out. Besides, hadn't Shīfù Hui told him he was supposed to pursue knowledge? So far, all he had managed to learn during his several months as a student in this place were little bits and pieces about the Dragon's Creed.

Even those things had taken a lot of effort to get his teacher to discuss. As before, the pattern for obtaining information from his teacher seemed clear. If Apollo wanted to learn the fourth part of the Creed, he would first have to demonstrate that he had mastered the third.

Apollo repeated that precept over and over again in his mind.

The head of a dragon must seek learning and knowledge throughout its entire life.

At first, Apollo attempted to do this honestly. His experience with Lanfen had taught him the importance of asking Shīfù Hui's permission before doing anything that might go contrary to an order that he had already been given. Hopeful that the same tactic would work again, Apollo approached his teacher one evening and asked him for permission to explore the upper levels of the school, explaining that he wanted to seek knowledge.

Apollo had expected Shīfù Hui to be proud of him. Pride had been the emotion his teacher had responded with the last time Apollo attempted to follow his teachings. On the evening when Apollo asked for permission to go upstairs, though, Shīfù Hui did not respond positively. Instead, he became visibly upset. For a few minutes, Apollo thought the man might even revoke his freedom and require Apollo to once again be escorted back to his room after meals.

When Shīfù Hui regained his composure, he grabbed Apollo sternly by the shoulders and made him repeat his promise that he would be obedient and never leave the basement for any reason.

Not wanting to further provoke his teacher's anger, Apollo vigorously nodded and reassured him that he would follow all his rules.

Once again, Apollo had given his promise in earnest and fully intended to honor his word. So much so that he did his very best over the next few days to set aside any desire to explore the rest of the building and instead focused on trying to find other ways that he could learn while remaining a prisoner underground.

Ultimately, though, it was his teacher's overreaction to his request that led Apollo back to his original plan.

Why had the man been so upset? Why was he so insistent that Apollo remain downstairs? Shīfù Hui's demeanor increased Apollo's curiosity exponentially. He constantly wondered what everyone did upstairs and why none of them wanted him to know about it.

Whatever the answers to these questions were, Apollo realized that the only way he would ever find out would be to do the one thing he had so ardently promised his teacher he would never do.

Apollo waited in his room until long after his usual bedtime. He wanted to be certain that everyone else in the building would be asleep. If he were caught down in the basement, it wouldn't be that big of a deal. He could just say that he had been going to the bathroom. A late-night trip to the restroom was something he had done more than once during his time at the school. However, Apollo had no ready excuse to use if someone found him wandering around upstairs.

When he felt confident that he had waited long enough, Apollo pushed the door of his room open and looked out into the hallway.

The candles were all extinguished, which meant that he would have to use the faint rays of moonlight from the small windows near the ceiling to navigate through the dark passageway.

Apollo's plan was to use the blue staircase again. If someone caught him, he wanted it to be Lei. He figured it would be better to face someone he already knew than a stranger who might be older or potentially more dangerous.

Apollo made his way to the bottom of the stairs and then began to ascend them. It was too dark for him to see any of the dragons painted along the walls, but he was pretty sure he could feel their eyes following his progress.

When he came to the place where the stairs curved toward the door at the top, Apollo's pace slowed a little. The last time he'd passed through this door, Lei had been waiting on the other side. Apollo rubbed his hands together, climbed the final few steps, and then reached out and pushed the door open.

The room, which was empty, appeared to be located in one of the four corners of the building and was lined on two sides with large windows. These windows allowed a lot more of the moon's light into the space, making it much brighter than either the basement or the stairwell had been.

Apollo walked over to one of the windows and looked outside. He was surprised to discover that the ground was covered in a thick blanket of fresh snow. There must have been more than two feet piled up across the village floor. The only other time in Apollo's life when he could ever remember having seen so much snow was when his mother had taken him snowboarding in the mountains.

As Apollo turned back around, his attention was drawn toward another exquisitely painted mural similar to the one in the stairway. Whoever painted the walls in this place was incredibly talented.

This one stretched out across most of the ceiling. In the center, there was a large white lotus flower surrounded by four dragons who appeared to be guarding the flower. In many ways, they reminded Apollo of the four-headed dragon that was painted on the little poster that he kept tucked away inside the blue book down in his bedroom.

Just like that drawing, two of these dragons depicted in the mural were breathing out fire, while the other two were growling and baring their teeth. The fire from one of the dragons was split into two flames, which extended outward from either side of its mouth, while the fire of a second dragon formed a single flame.

A third dragon held out his forelimb, with a sharp curving talon ready to strike down anyone who got too close to the flower, while the fourth dragon held both of its arms out as though it were about to grab something. The dragon breathing out a single flame, and the dragon with its talon extended each had scales, while the other two dragons had smooth skin.

Apollo looked around the rest of the room, which was almost entirely empty, except a few cabinets and some hand-painted posters hung along some of the blue walls.

On one of these walls, opposite from where Apollo had entered, there was a nest carved into a wooden frame above a wide, arching doorway.

Apollo walked toward and then underneath the nest, passing through the archway and into another, much larger room. One that was breathtakingly beautiful and that must have filled most of the space inside the building. Apollo tilted his head back as he walked out onto a lower balcony so that he could see the entire room, which was four stories high and had terraces surrounding each of the four levels.

The railings around each level were painted with distinct colors. The lowest one where Apollo was standing was blue. The second level was orange, the third was green, and the uppermost was painted white. Each terrace also had a staircase painted the same color that led toward the central floor. Besides these railings, the rest of the room was finished in a deep, glossy brown.

Apollo noticed that on each level there was an archway identical to the one he had just walked through. Which he assumed must lead to rooms similar to the one behind him.

This realization led to another more important one. It occurred to Apollo that the vast open room he was standing in must be located directly above the dining room, which meant that each of these rooms probably had a stairway, like the one in the blue room, that led back down to the basement.

Apollo opened a small gate in the railing of the blue balcony and then descended a couple of steps until he was standing on a sheet of finely polished wood that covered the entire central floor. If he had been wearing socks, the floor would have been very slippery. His bare feet had the opposite effect, though. They stuck to the floor, giving him tremendous traction. As he walked out toward the center of the room, Apollo slowly turned around, taking in the entire scene.

The most notable feature in the room was the ceiling, where four giant bronze statues of fearsome-looking dragons hung upside down around the figure of another lotus flower.

Apollo wondered how such massive objects could be hung from the ceiling. Each one was at least two or three times bigger than he was. Once again, these dragon statues were very similar to the painting in his book.

As Apollo looked down from the statues, something on the fourth floor caught his eye. There was a doorway with a large lotus flower painted above it. On either side of this door, two dragons had been painted that seemed to be waving to him—each one inviting Apollo to come upstairs and pass through the door.

Apollo hurried to the white staircase, which he followed up to the top level. From there, he walked around the outer edge of the balcony and over to the open doorway. When he passed through it, he found himself at the bottom of another staircase. Apollo followed these stairs, which brought him to a room at the top of the building, where he saw something that at last got him very excited. The room was a library.

On three of the four walls, there were windows through which Apollo could see the white rooftop of the school. The building, which he initially believed to have been only four stories high, actually turned out to be five, with the fifth floor consisting entirely of an extensive library filled with books and scrolls.

Row after row of shelves, which were themselves each full of what must have been thousands of old manuscripts. Apollo picked up some of them and flipped through the pages. But unfortunately, almost everything he opened contained nothing but illegible handwritten Chinese characters.

However, with so many books to look through, Apollo remained hopeful that if he kept looking, eventually, he would find something more useful. He moved from shelf to shelf—opening and inspecting each book. Until finally, after a few hours of digging, he picked up something that, for a second time that night, got him excited.

Tucked onto a high shelf near the back of the library, Apollo discovered a book bound in white leather that had a picture of a lotus flower imprinted in gold on the cover. Like so many other things Apollo had seen that night, this lotus flower was also being guarded by four dragons. Apollo was relieved to discover that the pages were filled with drawings and diagrams.

He could understand diagrams.

His relief at having found something so useful was, however, short-lived and quickly replaced by panic. Apollo looked at the window and realized that he had lost track of time. The sky was not as dark as it should have been. It wasn't quite morning yet, but the sun was beginning to rise. If anyone woke up before he returned to his room in the basement, he would be discovered out of bed.

Apollo held the book tightly in his hand and hurried back down the staircase and through the doorway on the fourth floor. He was surprised to see how much brighter the large central room had become.

In his haste to return to the basement, Apollo bumped into a small table which, after wobbling for a moment, toppled over onto its side. The sound echoed loudly across the entire room. Horrified, Apollo ran down the white staircase, across the floor of the large central room, and through the archway that led into the smaller blue room. From there, he continued down the blue staircase and then back to his own room in the basement.

Breathing heavily, Apollo hid the white book inside his pillowcase and then sat on his mat, where he waited for Shīfù Hui to come in and collect him for breakfast.

Chapter Nineteen

The first time that a child enters into the Dragon's Nest to fight for the honor of their Xué is a moment of great pride, one that these little nestlings never forget. The terror of having to defend themselves in front of their entire community, along with the exhilaration and honor of finally getting to face their first foe in battle. It is something that each inevitably cherishes throughout the rest of their lives. Both the great Shā-Shǔ and his childhood companion Ling wrote fondly about their own memories of these experiences. What sets them apart, though, is the fact that each of them faced an opponent that was much more deadly and far more powerful than is typical for such tender nestlings.
—The Book of the Wyvern Spirits

The children in her Leheqi had been practicing for about an hour, and Ling was exhausted when Qiao stopped and had them all sit down on the floor. Everyone moved quickly to their assigned places, forming four straight rows of sixteen children, with the youngest sitting in the front and the oldest in the back.

When they were all seated, Qiao began to address them—walking slowly back and forth around the room.

"Today will be a great day. The Dǎoshī has invited us into the Dragon's Nest for a Cháo zhàn."

During Ling's time in the Temple, she had already witnessed more than a dozen of these intense battles, which seemed to occur about once every week or two. During a Cháo zhàn, the entire Temple was expected to enter into the Dragon's Nest, where they all stood together on the balconies surrounding the central floor. Two Xué of roughly equal skill were then selected to fight against each other in a match that tested their skills as Dragons.

These battles always terrified Ling, especially when the competing Xué were made up of older nestlings. The younger children fought hard, but they weren't allowed to use weapons, and they weren't nearly as strong. In contrast, the older Xué not only fought with weapons, but they moved with incredible intensity and skill.

Because the competing Xué were evenly matched, a typical Cháo zhàn could last several minutes. Of course, the Dǎoshī always stopped these battles before anyone was killed, but injuries were common since both sides pressed each other hard, looking to take advantage of any weaknesses in their opponents.

There were very few rules in a Cháo zhàn. No one was allowed to begin until the Dǎoshī signaled for the match to start. She did this by having someone strike a large gong suspended above the railing on the bottom floor. Fighting would then continue until someone rang the gong a second time.

At any point during the match, either Xué could run over and ring the gong themselves, signifying that they had given up. But, of course, doing this meant accepting a dishonorable defeat.

Losing with honor required both sides to continue fighting until one side was so thoroughly overwhelmed by the other that the Dǎoshī had to extend mercy and end the match herself.

When a fight was over, it was then up to the Dǎoshī to decide who the winner was. Ling had yet to see a fight that didn't involve blood. Either because someone had been cut or, more often, because they had been given a bloody nose.

Considering how intense the battles became, Ling was not surprised that Qiao always did her best to motivate everyone beforehand, in case the Dǎoshī selected any of them to fight.

"If the Dǎoshī chooses our Leheqi for the great honor of showing off the strength of some of our Xué, then I expect whoever is selected to fight with spirit and heart."

This was the same lecture Qiao always gave them. Ling had heard it so often that she practically had it memorized.

"Within the walls of our training room, we are all brothers and sisters. But when we enter into the Nest, we are foes. You will not hold back just because you are friends. You will not show mercy just because you like each other. To show mercy in the Nest would bring dishonor to your Xué and our entire Leheqi."

Qiao's voice softened as she turned and looked at the children around her.

"Then, when the battle is over, we must leave our anger in the Nest. When we return to this room, we become friends again. No matter what happens on the floor of the Nest, here in this room, we remain united."

Even though she said it every time, Ling understood the importance of Qiao's words. So far, she had witnessed three battles between Xué from the Blue Engrow Leheqi. During one of these matches, a nine-year-old boy named Jinhai had attacked an eight-year-old girl named Jia. Jinhai had pulled Jia to the ground and then punched her hard in the side, causing her to scream out in pain. As he walked away, Jia spun around and dropped him to the floor. She then returned his punch, hitting him directly in the face. The two then spent the rest of the match chasing each other around the main floor. Each of them clearly furious with the other.

However, when the match had ended, and they returned to the safety of the group's training room, thanks to Qiao's intervention, they were able to set their anger aside and resume their friendship as though nothing had happened. Ling had to give credit to Qiao. She was very good at leading the rest of the group.

"Now, my Blue Engrows, you go through that door as Dragons. You are ready to attack any foe. No one can stop you. You are fearsome and dangerous. Go and show me how Dragons fight."

With that, everyone stood and walked under the archway and through the door that led into the Nest.

At each level, Ling could see the same thing occurring. Children in matching robes filed out of their respective doors and gathered around the balconies that overlooked the central floor.

Dǎoshī Xiai stood in the middle of the room, where she observed the Dragon nestlings as they entered quickly and orderly.

Once everyone was ready, the Dǎoshī held up her arms and began to speak.

"Huānyíng háizimen. Jīntiān wǒmen yào cānjiā bǐsài de dì yī wèi xuē jiāng shì dānshēn de lǜsè dàlìhuā."

Four boys wearing green robes quickly ran down the stairs from two balconies above and then stood to one side of the main floor, preparing themselves for battle.

An older Xué meant that weapons would be used during the match. Yue had explained to Ling that when a Xué graduated from

Orange Poppy to Green Dahlia, three members of that Xué were assigned to train in using a specific weapon, while the fourth member continued to specialize in hand-to-hand combat.

These weapons included the double-flame sword, the single-flame sword, and the dragon's talon. The handle of each flame sword resembled an elongated and slender dragon head, while the edges of the blade were jagged, resembling fire. When not in use, the tip of the blade retracted into the base, which then retracted down into the handle, reducing the length of each sword to a third of the original size so that these swords could more easily be concealed.

The dragon's talon was a short knife that curved like a claw and could be used to either hook or slice an opponent. It was razor-sharp on both sides of the blade so that any wounds inflicted against a foe would widen savagely as the weapon was withdrawn at an angle.

In addition to these weapons, both the wielder of the single-flame sword and the person who fought with the dragon's talon used their free hand to hold a dragon's scale fan, which consisted of a shield that folded up like a long fan when not in use. As with the flame sword, this design allowed the shield to be easily concealed underneath the bearer's clothing when it wasn't being used.

According to Yue, it was important for Dragons to always carry their weapons and armor wherever they went, even when doing the most mundane activities. Foldable swords and shields allowed a fully trained Xué to move throughout society with their armaments discreetly hidden but always readily available.

The unarmed member of a fully trained Xué represented the hands of the dragon. Their job was to throw opponents toward the other three or hold them while the others attacked. This individual was also a highly-skilled fighter. Without shields or weapons, though, they were more vulnerable to attack. However, united with the rest of their Xué, the dragon's hands became one of their most essential warriors.

Each Xué trained together throughout their entire childhood, learning to move as a single unit. By the time they were adults, they could practically read each other's minds, which is what made them so deadly. As they grew up together, they learned to communicate with grunts or by making eye contact. The only thing that could challenge a fully trained Xué in hand-to-hand combat was another fully trained Xué.

While the four Dahlias waited for the Dǎoshī to announce who their opponent would be, one of them reached down into two pockets that ran along the outside edges of his pants. From each of these pockets, the boy withdrew a flame sword.

With a sharp flick of his wrists, flame blades burst outward and clicked, locking into place. He then confidently swung the two swords around his arms while at the same time jumping into the air and kicking one of his feet out above him. The boy landed on his foot and immediately flung himself around backward into another flip, landing in a somersault. He then rolled back up to his feet and spun around in the other direction. The rest of his Xué also began to warm up, moving with the same precision and skill.

After a few moments, the Dǎoshī held up her arms. The four members of the Green Dahlia Xué immediately stopped and formed back into a straight line behind the Dǎoshī.

"Yǔ tāmen zuò dòuzhēng, wǒmen jiāng chéngwéi wǒmen de dì èr gè Xué."

Yanmei, who was standing just to the side of Ling, gasped audibly as both Qiao and Yue immediately began to run toward the gate that stood between the lower balcony and the main floor.

"Come on, Ling." Yanmei pulled her by the arm.

"I can't fight them. I can't fight anyone. I thought Dahlias were only supposed to fight against other Dahlias."

"The Dǎoshī can do whatever she wants. We have to go."

Ling wasn't even a match against the eight-year-olds in her own Leheqi. Every single one of them could easily defeat her. How was she supposed to fight against four muscular Dahlias?

"Yanmei, they will kill me," Ling barely managed to whisper.

"Better them than the Dǎoshī." Yanmei continued pulling Ling out and toward the floor, joining Qiao and Yue.

Ling wasn't sure what she would do first, pee her pants or throw up. Perhaps both at the same time. She instinctively crossed her legs and held her hand over her stomach.

Dǎoshī Xiai turned her head and smiled at Ling.

"I will now address you all in English so that everyone here may fully understand me. As many of you know, a few months ago, the ShI-Dǎoshī sent us a great gift. A chubby American girl who apparently possesses so much talent that she merited a place among our ranks without even passing the Lóng Tiǎozhàn. In fact, she is so talented that she took the place of one of your Dragon brothers, who had already trained for three years and who had earned his place among us."

As she spoke, her voice became louder and more aggressive.

"I think that someone with this much talent should be able to easily defeat an opponent as insignificant as a Green Dahlia Xué. Don't you?"

Dǎoshī Xiai then looked over at the boys who were standing behind her. "You will show these girls no mercy. I expect you to fight them as hard as you would fight any other Xué. Do you understand?"

They bowed to her.

"Good, now, let's make sure that this American girl has a chance to show off her talent. No one will be allowed to ring out of the battle. This fight will continue until I say that it's over."

With that, Dǎoshī Xiai exited the main floor and nodded for the gong to be rung.

The sound echoed off the walls and lingered in the air for several seconds. Immediately the four Green Dahlias began moving toward Qiao, Yanmei, Yue, and Ling.

"Form up," Qiao commanded.

Yanmei and Yue moved toward Qiao and stood with their backs together, leaving a gap on one side for Ling to join them.

"Ling. Form up. Now." Qiao shouted.

The Green Dahlias were quickly covering the distance between them. One of the boys lifted his sword so that he would be ready to swing down when he got within striking distance.

"LING!" Qiao shouted again.

Instead of joining the others, Ling abandoned them, running toward one of the four corners of the main floor. Her cowardice momentarily distracted their attackers, allowing Qiao to slide underneath one of the boys and sweep his legs, causing him to fall to the ground. As he went down, he dropped his dragon's scale fan, which Yanmei picked up. It wasn't much, but at least now they had something they could use to defend themselves.

Yanmei and Qiao rejoined Yue.

Yanmei did her best to protect all three of them with the shield, but her efforts did little good.

The three girls fought hard, but they were no match against four much older and more advanced Dragons. Even though they had only been fighting for a few seconds, all three were already bleeding from superficial wounds on their arms and legs.

"Wǒmen yào qiè chéng xiǎo fāngkuài, wǒmen xūyào sàn kāi bìng jiāng tāmen dāndú zhuāng shàng," Qiao shouted. "Xiànzài."

Immediately, all three girls split up, running toward the three unoccupied corners of the central floor. Each one of them pursued by one of the boys. Leaving the bearer of the dragon's talon to go after Ling.

The boy advanced toward Ling, holding his razor-sharp dragon talon in one hand and the dragon's scale fan in the other. When he got close, Ling hurried around him and began to run in the opposite direction. Once again, her cowardice surprised the boy. Giving Ling a head start as she fled.

Ling started to move toward Qiao, who she instinctively knew offered the best protection, but she stopped before reaching her. Qiao was already losing against her opponent.

Yanmei and Yue were doing even worse. Yanmei was crouched down, trying her best to hide behind the shield she had picked up, while Yue was being pulverized by the dragon's hands. If Ling joined any of them, she would bring another Green Dahlia with her, making their situation even worse.

Terrified and not knowing what else to do, she froze in the middle of the central floor.

Would Dǎoshī Xiai allow the boy to kill her on the floor of the Dragon's Nest? Probably not, but Ling knew the Dǎoshī would allow him to seriously injure her.

Ling suddenly realized that this had been the Dǎoshī's plan. To cause Ling so much physical harm that she would, at last, have an excuse to send her away. The Dǎoshī would then be able to tell the ShI-Dǎoshī that she had obeyed his orders, but unfortunately, the American girl had not been able to handle life in the Temple.

It would be a very convenient way to get rid of her. Ling would likely spend the rest of her life in a hospital, but everyone else in the Temple would then be able to go back to their normal routine.

Ling looked around the Nest desperately. On every level, hundreds of children watched as the Green Dahlia continued to close the gap between himself and her. Ling realized that if she wanted to survive, she would have to defend herself.

When the boy was just a few feet away, Ling's instincts took over. Instead of collapsing to the floor like she usually did during fights, she instead dove down hard into the boy's legs, causing the young man to lose his balance and fall forward. As he fell, he dropped his knife on the floor.

For just a moment, he lay face down, with the dragon's talon at his side. Ling remained on her hands and knees by the boy's feet. Still driven by instinct and acting out of a sense of self-preservation, she flung her entire body over the boy's legs. She reached out, grabbed the talon, and buried it deep into the boy's upper thigh.

The boy screamed as blood gushed out all over the floor. With each heartbeat, the red puddle grew larger. Ling had seen numerous wounds inflicted in the Nest before, but never one that resulted in so much blood so quickly. His entire pant leg had already turned red. Ling felt queasy. Her hands were sticky, and she could smell the blood. She bent over, and without meaning to, she threw up on the boy's head.

The Dǎoshī screamed something Ling couldn't hear, the gong rang out, and the match came to an end. The other three boys looked relieved and apologetic.

A couple of adults ran out onto the floor and pushed Ling aside. They grabbed the boy Ling had stabbed, ripped open his pants, and packed his gaping wound with a large amount of cotton cloth, which they stuffed directly into the opening of his gaping laceration. As one of them applied intense pressure to the boy's leg, another tied a tourniquet near his groin. The bleeding stopped, and the boy was carried out of the room.

The Dǎoshī looked impressed. Before dismissing everyone, she announced that Qiao, Yanmei, Yue, and Ling had won the match. All the children in the room erupted in applause. No one had ever seen a battle between two Xué who were so unevenly matched before. The fact that the Blue Engrows had won, when their defeat had been an absolute certainty, meant that the four girls were now instant celebrities within the Temple.

Ling went from being despised to being a hero in a single day. Qiao, Yanmei, and Yue were now bound to her. The victory brought their Xué together in a way that nothing else could have. It also unified the entire Leheqi around Ling.

Chapter Twenty

The poet-philosopher who we remember today as Héping jīngshén wrote some of the most memorable passages of her era on forgiveness and mercy. We know from accounts supposedly recorded by contemporaries of Ai-An that, while still a young girl, she spent at least some of her formative years as a student under the tutelage of this great savant. Whether or not this is true is less important than the fact that both Ai-An and Héping jīngshén shared the same beliefs on the eternal nature of humanity's ability to change for the better. That even the vilest of tyrants could, with proper guidance, become saints. Ai-An believed that when these "awakenings" occurred, they should be celebrated. And the newly "awakened" soul should then have all trust and respect restored to them. So few throughout history have replicated such sincerity of grace that it seems unlikely that Ai-An and Héping jīngshén could have inhabited the same era. What seems more likely to us is that Ai-An and the fabled Héping jīngshén were, in fact, the same person. After all, the practice of using pseudonyms was not uncommon during their lifetimes.
　　—The Book of the Wyvern Spirits

"Good morning, my Shā-Shŭ." It was very unusual for Shīfù Hui to greet Apollo so cheerfully.

"Good morning, Shīfù." Apollo bowed his head while instinctively glancing toward his pillowcase to make sure that the white book he had stolen a few days earlier was still out of sight.

"If you are ready, then let's go-to breakfast." Shīfù Hui waited for Apollo, which was also highly unusual. He was typically so much less patient.

As they walked side by side together, Shīfù Hui placed his hand on Apollo's shoulder. He didn't say anything, nor did he leave his hand there for very long, but the effect on Apollo was powerful. It filled him with a deep though momentary feeling of peace. Followed by an even greater sense of regret.

Apollo's unease had been steadily growing over the past few days. Ever since the night, he had explored the school. Now he just felt downright ashamed of himself. Shīfù Hui's expression of affection toward him was undeserved. His teacher had no idea how far Apollo had strayed from his promises, nor how much he had betrayed his trust.

As the two gathered their food, Shīfù Hui once again showed Apollo kindness by rubbing the back of his head. His teacher then headed off toward the adults' table, leaving Apollo to walk alone to his usual place against the wall.

Apollo's emotions must have been evident in the way he carried himself because as he passed Ai-An, she reached out and touched his hand. She looked genuinely concerned.

Instead of making him feel better, though, Ai-An's gesture added to his burden. He had been lucky to make friends with Ai-An and to have gained the trust of Shīfù Hui. Yet despite their kindness, Apollo had forsaken everything that both of them stood for.

What made Apollo feel even worse was that he was pretty sure if he had to do it over again, he would. What kind of a person was he? To know that something was wrong and to regret having done it, while deep down knowing that he would do it again if he had to?

Betraying the trust of those he loved was apparently a price Apollo was willing to pay as long as it meant getting what he wanted. Which Apollo was pretty sure made him a terrible person.

At the end of breakfast, as the children were lining up, Ai-An once again swung around the edge of the room so that she would pass by Apollo.

"Shā-Shǔ, your friends love you." She reached out her hand and gently brushed it against his forehead. She had been impressively discreet. No one else noticed that she had either spoken to or touched him. He, on the other hand, both heard and felt her.

What Ai-An was really saying was that she loved him since she was his only real friend there. She probably wouldn't say that, though, if she knew how he had betrayed his word.

After everyone left the dining room, Apollo stood up, wiped his eyes on his shirt, and then went to work cleaning up the dishes. After a few minutes, he was joined in his work by the old woman. During Apollo's short time as Lanfen's assistant, he had never spoken to her. Instead, their communications had always been through a series of gestures and nods.

Shīfù Hui had once told Apollo that everyone in the school spoke English. However, he had no idea if this also included people like Lanfen, who didn't have dragon tattoos.

After gathering the dishes from off the tables and carrying them back into the kitchen, Apollo filled the sink with water using a small hand pump located just above and a little behind the basin. Apollo glanced over at the gentle and harmless-looking woman as he cranked the pump up and down. She was sitting at a table a short distance from him, peeling potatoes.

"Lanfen?"

She looked up at him with the same amused expression she had worn on her face on the day when Apollo had first started helping her.

"Yes, Shā-Shŭ?" Her voice sounded warm and patient.

"You do speak English." he said, relieved.

"Everyone in the village speaks English." She smiled as she turned back to her potatoes.

"Why does everyone in the village speak English? Where are we? What is this place?"

Lanfen's easy nature helped Apollo to let his guard down. Which, in turn, resulted in all of his questions spilling out of him at once.

Lanfen listened patiently, waiting for Apollo to finish talking. When he did, she answered him.

"You are in Daletezhen, China. Everyone here speaks English because it is necessary. This place is the Yuándīng Temple."

It was refreshing to have someone willing to answer his questions so openly.

"What do you mean, speaking English is necessary?"

"It is necessary for our work."

"What is your work?"

"My work is to peel potatoes. Your work is to wash dishes." She chuckled.

"You have to speak English to peel potatoes?" Apollo looked at her doubtfully.

"Not everyone here peels potatoes, Shā-Shǔ." The woman smiled but didn't elaborate any further.

"What do they do?"

"They do what the Dǎoshī tells them to." Once again, she smiled warmly.

Dǎoshī was a word Apollo had never heard anyone use before. "What is the Dǎoshī?" he asked.

"Not what, but who. The Dǎoshī is Shi Ju-Long. Dǎoshī is not his name, but his title. Just like 'Shīfù' is the title you use when speaking to my son Hui."

"You are Shīfù Hui's mother?" Apollo let go of the plate he had been scrubbing, causing it to splash in the sink.

"Sorry," he apologized, grabbing a towel to clean up the mess he had made.

"Someone has to be his mother." she teased.

Apollo stood back up and continued washing the dishes. Before he could stop himself, Apollo asked the woman another question.

"Lanfen, what if somebody did something wrong so that they could learn how to do what they hoped was right?" Apollo kept his eyes focused on his dishes. He hadn't meant for this to become a confession. He could feel Lanfen studying him. After a few moments, she spoke again, using the same sweet voice she had employed before.

"Sometimes, Shā-Shǔ, the rules are clear, and it is easy to know what we are supposed to do. But, other times, everything feels much more murky, like your dirty dishwater.

"We might think that what we are doing is right when the

truth is that we are actually on the wrong path. Or we might think that we have done something wrong when our actions were proper and honorable.

"It is not for me to decide whether the conduct of another person was right or whether it was wrong. That is between them and the Wyvern Spirits. But remember, things are not always as clear as they seem or as concrete as you have perhaps been taught."

"What is a Wyvern spirit?" Apollo hoped he wasn't annoying Lanfen, but he couldn't help himself.

"You ask a lot of questions, don't you?" Lanfen smiled. "Well, when we die, if we have lived an honorable life, then our spirits transform into wyverns or dragons." Lanfen held out her arms as though she were soaring through the air. "We get to spend the rest of eternity exploring the universe and helping the mortals along their many journeys in this world."

"So what's right and wrong is between myself and a bunch of dead dragons?" he asked incredulously.

Lanfen laughed. "I suppose that is one way to put it." She sat down her potatoes and walked over to where Apollo was working. "Shā-Shŭ, who are your Wyvern Spirits?"

Apollo wasn't sure how to answer her.

"Who has crossed over from life into eternity? Who are your ancestors?"

Apollo thought for a moment and then answered resolutely, "My mother."

Lanfen looked genuinely sad for Apollo. She reached out and took Apollo's hand in her own.

"Oh, my poor boy, losing your mother at such a young age would be hard. But you are lucky. A maternal Wyvern Spirit is the most powerful kind. Some spirits leave the world and fly far away, neglecting their descendants. But a mother never flies very far from her child. Her instincts are too strong. Your mother is always nearby, Shā-Shǔ."

Lanfen squeezed Apollo's hand reassuringly before continuing.

"She wields her fire to protect you. And if you listen carefully, sometimes you will hear her whisper. Sometimes she will give you advice. If that advice leads you away from what others might be telling you to do, then you must have the wisdom to follow her."

"What if the person I disobeyed was your son?" Apollo asked uncertainly.

"My son Hui is a good man. There is much that he can teach you. But Shā-Shǔ, the people of this village, have a strong tradition based on strict and absolute obedience. Sometimes they take things a little too seriously when following orders. Which is probably why I peel potatoes instead of serving as the Dǎoshī."

Lanfen then unexpectedly laughed and shook her head. "Follow my son; his heart is true. But when your own Wyvern Spirits whisper to you and guide you to go down some other path, you must listen to them also and not waste any time feeling guilty about it."

Chapter Twenty-One

In the ancient manuscript entitled 'The Memoirs of Jiàn Hui: To Teach a Master,' we find the account of another curious miracle performed by the great Shā-Shǔ, wherein he demonstrated his ability to read and interpret unfamiliar languages. Did he accomplish this feat through the use of cleverness and supposition, or did the Wyvern Spirits indeed bless him with the ability to read and understand foreign dialects?

Rumors of his ability to translate languages are common, all of which have their roots in this account as recorded in his teacher's own writing. It is evident from these records that at least insofar as Jiàn Hui was concerned, his student did indeed have the ability to interpret languages. Therefore, we can see no reason to counter the claims of this contemporary eyewitness.

—The Book of the Wyvern Spirits

Though he didn't fully understand what Lanfen had meant about the difference between right and wrong, Apollo's conversation with the old woman still made him feel better. With the burden of his guilt now eased, Apollo found himself anxious to begin studying the white leather book that he had taken from the library on the fifth floor.

Between meals, and whenever Apollo was absolutely sure no one else would interrupt him, he spent his time skimming through the book's pages. It took some time, but eventually, he began to make sense of the figures and drawings.

The book was divided into four sections, each of which was marked by a different-colored flower. The first roughly one-fourth of the book had tiny blue flowers hand-painted in the bottom right corner of each page. The next one-fourth of the book had orange flowers, the third section had green flowers, and the final quarter had white flowers.

The pages contained figures of people performing what looked like advanced dance moves. Toward the end of the book, these dancers held weapons, such as swords, shields, and curved knives.

In many ways, the diagrams reminded Apollo of the dragons painted on the blue staircase, which started near the bottom of the stairs looking as though they were dancing, but then by the time they reached the top of the stairs, they became fearsome and dangerous. He wondered if this was what Ai-An had meant when she talked to him about the dance of the dragons. Some sort of dance that evolved into fighting?

Apollo flipped through the book page by page. In the beginning, the moves were simple enough, nothing beyond the skill level of an experienced gymnast like Apollo. But as he continued through the book, the figures became far more complex, illustrating maneuvers that looked extremely difficult. Apollo didn't see how any normal human could perform actions like those depicted in the final section. Especially not while holding swords in their hands, as some of the people in the drawings were.

Having nothing else to occupy his time, Apollo began on the first page. It was impossible to know whether or not he was doing the forms correctly, but he did the best he could.

When he wasn't practicing or helping Lanfen in the kitchen, Apollo exercised. He did push-ups, sit-ups, crunches, and stretches. Some of the more advanced moves depicted toward the back of the first section would require greater strength than Apollo currently had. If he were going to master these moves, he would have to start preparing his body now.

His natural flexibility and the fact that he had done gymnastics for more than half his life allowed Apollo to quickly advance through the first several pages. After only a few weeks, he had become rather adept at performing the maneuvers outlined in the first ten pages. His body increased in both strength and endurance as well.

Unfortunately, Apollo found it challenging to move beyond these first ten pages though. Many of the moves depicted after that point required a lot of movement. Something that just wasn't possible in his tiny room. He needed to find somewhere else to practice.

The large open room in the center of the building would have been perfect, though he would have been equally happy with one of the smaller rooms, such as the one at the top of the blue staircase. He briefly considered sneaking up there at night but quickly dismissed that idea as far too risky. He might be able to get away with tiptoeing around upstairs, but there was no way he would be able to run, flip, and occasionally fall without someone hearing him.

With no other options, Apollo focused primarily on his muscle strength, flexibility, and the forms outlined on the first ten pages. However, he also spent a lot of time studying the other pages.

He might not have enough room to practice the movements outlined in the rest of the book, but he could at least imagine himself going through their motions in his mind. As he did so, Apollo began to unintentionally memorize the entire book.

Which only made his desire to practice the advanced moves all the more frustrating. After wrestling with the problem on his own for several weeks, Apollo decided to once again seek advice from the only person in the school who he knew he could talk to freely.

In the few months since he had confessed to Lanfen that he had done something wrong, she had never betrayed his trust by telling either Shi Ju-Long or her son about their conversation. Instead, she had been faithful and loyal in keeping his secret.

Apollo decided that it was time to confide in her again. So one evening, after finishing the dishes, Apollo sat down on one of the stools in front of the small table by the wall. He took a deep breath, gathering both his thoughts and his courage. Lanfen watched him kindly from across the room but didn't say anything. Instead, she waited patiently for Apollo to be ready to speak on his own.

"I have a problem, and I don't know what to do." Apollo blurted out awkwardly.

Lanfen didn't laugh or belittle the way Apollo had spit out the words. Instead, she nodded encouragingly to him.

"If I tell you about my problem, I am going to get in a lot of trouble."

"Who is going to get you in trouble?" Lanfen glanced around the room. "The potatoes?"

"No." Apollo couldn't help but smile. "Not the potatoes. Your son. If he knew what I have done or what I am thinking about doing again, he would be upset with me."

Lanfen walked over to Apollo and sat down on the stool next to him. She dried her hands on her apron and then took one of Apollo's hands and held it with both of hers.

"It sounds like you are carrying a great weight, Shā-Shŭ. The best way to ease a heavy burden is to share it with someone else." She patted his hand with hers. "Whatever you tell me will stay between us." She winked at him. "Unless one of the potatoes talks. You never know with potatoes." She smiled.

Apollo explained to Lanfen that all he had wanted to do was follow the teachings of Shīfù Hui in living up to the third precept of The Dragon's Creed. He told her about how his efforts to seek knowledge led him to sneak up to the top of the Temple, where he had discovered the library and stolen a book.

Throughout his confession, Lanfen's kind nature helped keep Apollo feeling comfortable and at ease, which resulted in him spilling detail after detail until he told her pretty much everything.

When he was done, he turned and looked at her, waiting to hear how she would respond after finding out all that he had done.

"You have shown great courage, Shā-Shŭ."

Apollo looked at her doubtfully. He had just confessed breaking pretty much every rule he had been given. Apollo wondered if perhaps the woman had somehow misunderstood him.

"What?" she asked. "You don't think it takes courage to do what you have done? To try your best to do what you think is right, or to do things that carry great risk. That is the very definition of courage."

"But I stole something." Apollo shifted uncomfortably in his seat.

"Are you going to give the book back?" she asked him.

"Um, I hadn't really thought about that. I guess I can."

"Good. Then it isn't stealing, is it? It's just borrowing. Shā-Shŭ, the Lotus Room is a library. The records are there for anyone who lives in the Temple. Which technically includes you. So borrowing the book wasn't stealing.

"Anyway, let's talk about your other problem. You need a place to practice, correct?"

"Yes. My room is too small, and I am not allowed to go upstairs. I want to get better, but I can't do it in the basement."

Lanfen was now smiling broadly, making her look much younger.

"It has been too long since I have enjoyed the pleasure of breaking some rules." She sighed thoughtfully.

Apollo wondered how Lanfen and Shīfù Hui could be related. He was always so strict and conforming, whereas this woman was downright giddy with delight at the possibility of helping Apollo subvert the rules.

"Shā-Shŭ. Can't you see that we have the perfect place for you right here?"

"In the kitchen?" Apollo looked around. The kitchen was larger than his room, but it was filled with tables, shelves, and counters. There wasn't very much open floor space.

"No, not in the kitchen. In the dining room."

She stood up, looking genuinely excited.

"Each night after dinner, you and I will push all of the tables to the side of the room. If anyone asks, I will just tell them that I am cleaning the floors. When I leave to go to bed, I will pass by your bedroom door and knock, letting you know that it is safe for you to come out. Wait another five minutes and then head to the dining room, where you will have all the space you need to practice. Each morning, we will return the tables to their proper order. No one will suspect a thing."

"Won't they hear me practicing?"

"Who is going to hear you?"

"I don't know. Whoever else sleeps down here in the basement."

"You and I are the only ones who sleep in the basement. Everyone else sleeps on their assigned floors upstairs. There is no one else down here at night."

"How will I help you move the tables back? I have to wait in my room until Shīfù Hui comes to get me for breakfast."

"That's a good point. Let's see. " Lanfen sat down. "I will tell my son that I need your help in the mornings and that if he wants to be kind to his aging mother, he will allow you to come to the dining room earlier and on your own."

Lanfen's plan went pretty much as she had predicted. Together they moved the tables off to the side of the room each evening after dinner and then moved them back in the morning before anyone else arrived for breakfast. Shīfù Hui still retrieved Apollo for lunch and dinner, but Apollo was now allowed to go to the dining room on his own for breakfast.

At night, when Apollo was alone in the dining room, he had more than enough space to practice.

At first, he tried to keep his noise level to a minimum. However, he soon discovered that it really didn't matter how loud he was. More than once, he got a little carried away and ended up crashing into a wall, or worse, knocking over a table.

The first time this happened, Apollo had been terrified that someone might have heard him. But his fears proved to be unwarranted. The stone walls were just too thick, and everyone else was too far away. He probably could have yelled at the top of his lungs without drawing any of their attention to him.

In time Apollo reached the point where he no longer needed to refer to the book. Instead, he could close his eyes and see every single figure and form perfectly. He knew them as well as he knew the alphabet, or how to count from one to ten.

He had promised Lanfen that he would return the book to the Lotus Room when he no longer needed it. In the end, though, they decided that it would be safer for her to return it. Lanfen told Apollo that if anyone asked her why she had borrowed the book, she would just pretend that she had no idea what they were talking about and act as though she were senile, a comment which made both of them laugh.

The weeks began to pass much more quickly now that Apollo had fully engaged himself in something that was both fun and challenging. He looked forward to his evening practice sessions. He enjoyed seeing how much further he could push himself each night, and it was gratifying to feel his body growing stronger.

After three months of hard work, Apollo completely mastered the entire first section. He then began working on combining the forms together. Realizing that if he performed them in the order they appeared in the book, he could flow through them effortlessly.

They were designed so that when he finished the first form, his hands and feet were already precisely where they needed to be to start the second. After another month of practice, Apollo found that he could fluently transition through the entire series in the blue section without making any mistakes at all.

Chapter Twenty-Two

It would be unwise for us to judge the actions of Ling as having been either good or evil, right or wrong. Instead, we must remember that the path that stretched out in front of her from the very moment of her birth was already treacherous. Could any of us have done better had we found ourselves in her shoes? Indeed, although it is true that until she was killed in the battle of Zuìhòu de dòuzhēng, Ling committed many acts that caused others to experience tremendous suffering, but her destiny cannot be separated from that of the Shā-Shŭ. For without the one, history would have been deprived of the other.
—*The Book of the Wyvern Spirits*

"Ah, Shun, please sit down." Tan Far gestured toward a chair in front of his desk.

Shun's flight from China had landed only a few hours earlier, and this late-night meeting was the first time that Tan Far had ever talked to the man. He looked young and unsure of himself. The way he squirmed in his chair reminded Tan Far of a child.

A few weeks earlier, Far had put a call out to the leaders of all his Dragon villages asking that they find him a Xué capable of smuggling something of great value from China back to the United States.

Shun and his Xué had been enthusiastically recommended by their Dǎoshī, who claimed that the four of them could disappear and reappear on demand. He compared them to ghosts and promised Tan Far that he would not be disappointed in their abilities.

Tan Far leaned back against the front edge of his desk and inspected the man more carefully. "Has Meili filled you in on the situation with the young man in China?"

Shun nodded nervously.

The man's weakness repulsed Tan Far. However, their mission would require stealth, not strength. Far trusted the Dǎoshī who had recommended them, and anyway, weasels like Shun usually made the best smugglers. Moreover, his nervousness would make him better at hiding.

"Good. Take your Xué and travel to the village where he is being held. I want you to bring him here to me, alive."

"Shì de wǒ de zhǔ," Shun answered, nodding.

"Shun, Perhaps no one told you, but we speak only English when we are in America." Tan Far looked at his guest disapprovingly.

"I sorry, English, not how good as I like."

Tan Far stood up and walked around and then behind the man, feeling even more disgusted by him. Speaking English was one of the primary responsibilities of a Dragon. Apparently, his Dǎoshī didn't think it was important enough to mention to Far that the man had neglected his language skills. He would have to deal with this Dǎoshī later.

"But my smuggle good." The man nodded stupidly.

"Just bring me the young man." Tan Far paused and then added, "Keep him alive, Shun. When you return, I will be performing an execution. If he is not with you, or if he is already dead, then that execution will be yours."

One of the benefits of owning a deli was that Tan Far had access to many tools perfectly designed for cutting up and disposing of meat.

Shun bowed a second time.

Far turned and walked around his desk. Pausing to look out the window at the streetlights below his home. After a moment, he realized that he hadn't heard Shun leave. Tan Far turned back around, but the man was gone. Despite his dislike for Shun, Far had to admit, he really did move like a ghost.

Ling had spent most of her young life believing that the world was a very different place from how she now understood it actually was. She used to think that what mattered were celebrities, memes, buying pretty outfits, and spending as much time as possible with her best friend, Apollo.

However, the more time she spent training as a Dragon, the more she realized how superficial and shallow her life had once been. Discovering her heritage and connection to the village of Xitanxiang had given Ling a new purpose. She was gradually becoming aware that honor and self-fulfillment came through obedience to something greater than herself.

Ling tried not to think about the weak and lonely girl she had once been. That girl no longer existed. The old Ling was gone. A new and much stronger girl had blossomed in her place, one who understood that she was not just any other typical teenage girl. She was a Dragon.

Ling used to believe she was nothing more than the daughter of Tan Far, a man who owned and operated a local deli in San Francisco, California. Now, though, she understood that while she was still Tan Far's daughter, he was much more than just the shopkeeper of a local restaurant. Instead, he was the head of the Dragon Order, a worldwide network consisting of dozens of villages like where she presently lived. Each village with a Temple operated and staffed by many worthy and powerful Xué. All of whom were loyal to him.

Whenever anyone spoke of her father, it was always with respect and admiration. They spoke of how good, wise, and noble he was. That he was the most impressive ShI-Dǎoshī in nearly two thousand years, and of how he was leading the Dragon Order to greater stature than any other ShI-Dǎoshī had ever done before him.

No one knew that Ling was Tan Far's daughter. He had expressly forbidden Niu from revealing this secret, and out of respect for her father, she had chosen to honor this command as well. Even if she had claimed him as her father, she doubted that anyone would believe her. Ling knew who she was, though, and she was proud. Her father was the most important Dragon of all time. His blood flowed through her veins, which, as far as Ling was concerned, had to count for something.

Her newfound self-confidence was further bolstered by her friendship with the rest of her Xué. Qiao, Yanmei, and even Yue had all become sisters to her. They loved and accepted Ling as a full member who belonged to them. Together the three of them had spent hundreds of hours working hard to help Ling improve over the past few months.

Under their careful guidance, she had progressed rapidly. All of this additional practice had another effect as well. She began to lose weight and was now much skinnier than she could ever remember being. She could now easily touch her toes, as well as lift her foot high up above her head. When she first arrived in the Temple, Ling would get winded after just a few minutes of practice. Now, though, she could go through an entire four-hour session without having to stop and rest a single time.

Though she still had a long way to go before she caught up to the rest of her Leheqi, Ling was determined that someday, like her father, she, too, would become the very best among them. She knew that she would ultimately even surpass Qiao and take her place as the Qiān-lóng of their Leheqi.

Ling couldn't help but wonder what Apollo would think of her if he could see what she was becoming. It had now been nearly a year since the two of them had talked to each other. During that time, her love for Apollo hadn't lessened at all. Even now, she still wore his dìnghūn coin around her neck.

Ling knew that she and Apollo would probably never see each other again, but if they did, she hoped that they would be able to pick up their friendship where they had left off. She could then show him how much she had changed. For now, though, she would content herself with her training.

Today Qiao had them working on a move where they were supposed to block their opponent's with both arms crossed in front and above their heads while simultaneously stepping backward and then to the side, causing their opponent to trip and collapse onto the ground. It was fun, though extremely challenging, especially considering that here in the Blue Engrow training room, each opponent knew in advance exactly what to expect. While she wasn't as successful as anyone else, she did manage to drop a few of the younger children.

They practiced for about ninety minutes when Dǎoshī Xiai entered their training room. Before the Dǎoshī could take more than three steps through the door, every single child stopped what they were doing and, without being asked, immediately lined up in front of her, making four rows consisting of sixteen children each.

A few seconds later, a fully realized Xué, made up of two adult men and two adult women, entered the room dragging with them a much older woman who looked panic-stricken. One of the men picked the woman up and stood her on her feet in front of the children.

The woman's worn skin stretched tightly across her skinny arms and legs. She shook from the effort it took to remain standing without anything to support her weight. Ling wanted to find the woman a cane or something else that she could use to hold on to, but she knew better than to move out of her place while the Dǎoshī was watching.

After standing the woman on her feet, the fully realized Xué retreated a few steps. The Dǎoshī then stepped forward and turned her attention to the perfectly straight rows of Blue Engrows.

"This is Dù Yan. Many of you will undoubtedly recognize her from the village. She has worked alongside some of your parents in the flour mill for many years. Some of your parents are probably even friends with her.

"Dù Yan has acted with deceit. She has been stealing from the rest of us to enrich herself. This Xué discovered her taking flour from the mill and bringing it home to her own family without permission. She is unworthy of living with our people any longer. Before she is thrown out of the village, though, she must be punished. I have brought her to you, my budding Engrows. How will you punish her?"

Dǎoshī Xiai paused long enough to look around the room. She then turned to Qiao. "How will you punish her, Qiao?"

Qiao looked uncomfortable, but she didn't hesitate to answer. "The law says that she must be beaten for her crime, Shīfù."

Dǎoshī Xiai nodded approvingly and gestured toward the woman with an open palm. "Let's have Ling do it."

Qiao bowed to her and then quickly walked over to the wall where they kept various training supplies in a cabinet. She opened the door and retrieved a bamboo staff about the length and thickness of a broomstick. Qiao then returned to where Ling was standing and handed the staff to her.

Ling glanced at the frail pitiful looking woman. There was no way the woman could withstand something so cruel as being beaten by a bamboo staff. Nor did Ling think that she would be capable of inflicting such brutal harm against someone so defenseless.

"Ling, you must strike her. She's only a lotus flower. She deserves to be punished." Yue sounded very sure of herself, but Ling didn't share that certainty. No one deserved to be brutalized by a bamboo staff, least of all an elderly woman who could barely stand.

Ling looked around the room, pleading. "I can't hurt her." she said softly, dropping the bamboo staff onto the floor.

"If you will not perform your duty, child, then you will be beaten alongside her. Not just by one person, but by everyone in this room." The Dǎoshī's words were spoken very matter-of-factly.

Ling again scanned the room. She looked into the faces of several members of her Leheqi. Each person she looked at nodded their encouragement and support. Ling reasoned that it would be better for her to strike the woman herself with a single blow than to have both her and the woman get beaten by multiple blows from everyone else.

Ling bent down and retrieved the bamboo staff. She slowly walked over to the woman and lifted the staff above her head. Ling closed her eyes and then brought the staff down hard. As it swung through the air, the bamboo made a wheezing sound. When it struck the woman across her shoulders, she stumbled forward, but to Ling's relief, she didn't completely collapse.

"Excellent, Ling. You are finding your place here. But I don't think that was your best effort, was it? I think you can strike Dù Yan harder."

The Dǎoshī was right. Ling had held back out of mercy for the woman, which was not what the Dǎoshī wanted to see. Ling realized that she would make her strike the woman repeatedly until she did it right. Better to get it over with now than to have to assault the poor woman over and over again.

Ling lifted her arm again, and this time swung down with all her strength. The woman whimpered and fell backward to the floor.

"One more time, Ling."

Ling closed her eyes again. It was horrible. She was horrible. When her third blow struck, the woman barely even made a noise. She just lay on the floor, breathing unsteadily.

"Very good. You may return to the line." Dǎoshī Xiai then turned to face the Xué who had brought the old woman into the room. "Take her out into the wilderness and leave her there. She is never to be allowed in our village again."

All four members of the Xué bowed and then dragged the woman out of the room. Dǎoshī Xiai immediately followed behind them, leaving the children alone.

Yue was the first to speak.

"It's not your fault, Ling. Dù Yan was disobedient, and disobedience merits the greatest punishment of all."

"I always thought she was such a nice woman," whispered Yanmei. "Dù Yan used to bring my mother and me extra bread when we didn't have enough to eat." Yanmei's face suddenly looked alarmed, and she quickly added, "Of course, we had no idea that she was stealing the flour. We thought she was giving it to us from her own supply."

Qiao rolled her eyes. "Don't worry, Yanmei, everyone here knows that your father was a hero. No one is going to suspect your family of being in league with Dù Yan." She then walked over to where Ling was standing and gently pulled the bamboo staff out of her tightly held grip. Ling didn't move.

"Ling, you made the right choice." Qiao's words were spoken much more softly than Ling had ever heard her speak before. "The Dǎoshī isn't someone who changes her mind. If you didn't obey her, your punishment would have been even worse than Dù Yan's."

Yanmei walked over and joined them, dragging Yue along with her. The three of them held Ling in their arms as she leaned into their hug and sobbed.

Chapter Twenty-Three

Just as the Yin has its counter in the Yang, with both being equally balanced against one another, so, too, were the Shā-Shŭ and his greatest enemy, who history sometimes refers to as the Panda Wraith. Each pushed back against the other. Therefore, it would be impossible for this or any other historian to attempt to write the biography of the Shā-Shŭ' without also mentioning the tyrannical deeds of his childhood companion.
—The Book of the Wyvern Spirits

"Shā-Shŭ, can you follow me please."

Lunch had just ended, and Apollo was cleaning up one of the tables when his teacher entered the dining room and approached him from behind. Apollo immediately sat down the stack of plates he was holding and turned to face him.

"Yes, Shīfù," Apollo answered, bowing his head. "Where are we going?"

"You have been in the basement for too long, my Shā-Shŭ. You need sunlight."

They left the dining room together, walked down a hallway, up a set of stairs, and then into the Temple foyer, where Shīfù Hui gave Apollo a pair of sandals. From there, they exited through one of the doors and out onto the porch.

Apollo remembered the Sun, but he had forgotten how bright it could be. The snow that Apollo had seen several months earlier was now all completely melted, replaced by a blanket of thick green grass, flowers, and butterflies.

Even the air was better outside. In the basement, it was cold, stale, and musty. Whereas out here, it felt warm and smelled like flower blossoms and grass.

Unless Shīfù Hui planned to allow him to come outside every day, Apollo almost wished that he hadn't brought him up at all. It would take weeks for Apollo to settle back into his routine, knowing there was so much sunshine just a few steps away from his bedroom door.

That didn't keep Apollo from enjoying every second of their walk together right now, though. Apollo breathed in deeply. Hoping to fill his lungs with as much of the fresh air as possible, and his mind with the sound of chirping birds, the deep blue color of the sky, and the way the sunshine felt on his face. He imagined himself letting out this breath later, once he had returned to his room, perhaps bringing a few of these things back down into the dark basement with him.

"Come here, my Shā-Shŭ." Shīfù Hui began to walk down the front steps of the Temple and then around toward the side.

"Do you believe in destiny?" Shīfù Hui spoke quietly, sounding reflective.

"You mean like fate?"

"Yes, I suppose fate is another word in English that means almost the same thing."

"My mother believed in fate," Apollo admitted, though he wasn't sure if he fully understood what the word meant or whether or not he shared her beliefs.

"That is good, Shā-Shǔ. You should trust your ancestors." Shīfù Hui patted Apollo on his shoulder. Then, as they continued walking, he pulled Apollo into a brief side hug. Apollo leaned his head up against Shīfù Hui's shoulder. It was a powerful gesture that both of them needed and enjoyed.

They walked toward the back of the Temple and entered a beautifully manicured garden. Inside this garden, there was a large pond filled with what looked like oversized orange-and-white goldfish. On the surface of the pond, a couple of swans lazily floated toward the shade of a tree. As Apollo and Shīfù Hui wandered through the garden, they passed several children walking together in their usual groups of four.

"Shā-Shǔ, I also believe in destiny. I believe that you have suffered many difficulties during your time here, but you have worked hard, and you have made me very proud. I do not know your destiny, but I believe you will have the strength to face whatever challenges may soon come to you. Do you understand?"

Apollo did not understand, but he didn't want to disappoint Shīfù Hui, so he nodded politely.

Satisfied, Shīfù Hui turned and began to meander toward the far side of the gardens. They walked past a long hedge that was about two feet high and then through a gate that led out into the village. From there, Shīfù Hui led Apollo up one of the two main streets and then down a smaller side road.

After walking for about twenty minutes, Shīfù Hui stopped in front of a small home with a faded blue roof. Pausing briefly, Shīfù Hui looked around and then nervously asked Apollo to follow him inside. Once inside, they walked to the back of the house, where they entered into the smaller of two bedrooms. Shīfù Hui sat down on a stool near one of the walls.

Shīfù Hui remained silent as he turned his head and slowly took in the room. Out of respect for his teacher, Apollo pretended not to notice the emotions welling up in the man's face.

"This was my son's room." Shīfù Hui cleared his throat and briefly closed his eyes before continuing, "He was a very good boy, Shā-Shŭ, just like you. A very good boy."

Apollo hadn't realized Shīfù Hui had a son. Neither he nor Lanfen had ever mentioned anything about him before.

"Is he one of the students in the school?" Apollo realized too late that Shīfù Hui had spoken of his son in the past tense.

Shīfù Hui looked up at Apollo with painfully heavy eyes. "My son is now a Wyvern Spirit. He was taken from this world due to mistakes made a long time ago by his father. It would seem that the Jiàn family has a history of being headstrong when following the law. My mother has always been obstinate, I have at times been that way, and unfortunately, my son also inherited this part of our family's character."

Apollo didn't know what to say, so he remained silent while Shīfù Hui collected his thoughts.

"Anyway, my Shā-Shŭ, I brought you here because I want to give you something so that you will always remember me."

Shīfù Hui stood up and walked over to a small cabinet against one of the walls. He opened the front cupboard door and pulled out a beautiful white sheet of flowing silk. The top of the silk cloth was embroidered with red, orange, and yellow flames, while the rest was covered in a pattern that resembled scales.

"This is my family's Dragon cloak. It is a ceremonial robe

usually passed down from father to son. A father presents it to his son only after a boy has proven himself worthy to carry on the family's name. Shā-Shǔ, you have proven yourself worthy. You have shown that you are ready to live as an honorable man."

Shīfù Hui instructed Apollo to turn around. He draped the dragon cloak over Apollo's shoulders and buttoned it up around his neck.

Apollo felt uncomfortable. This was the most meaningful gift anyone had ever offered him. He wasn't sure it would be appropriate though to take something so sacred from Shīfù Hui's family. Nor did he feel worthy of the gesture. He was about to take it off when Shīfù Hui placed his hand on Apollo's shoulder.

"It's okay, Shā-Shǔ. I'll feel better knowing that you have it with you than if it is sitting here gathering dust. My line has ended. I will have no more sons. I want to pass this cloak on to you." Shīfù Hui sounded like he might say something more, but his words were choked off, and he went silent instead.

Apollo looked at himself in a large mirror leaning up against one of the walls. The cloak was stunningly beautiful. It flowed like billowing fire in the wind as he turned.

"The dragon cloak is sacred, my Shā-Shǔ. It calls out to our Wyvern Spirit ancestors. Those Wyvern Spirits who care most about us are drawn in around us when we wear it. We can then more easily hear their voices and communicate with them.

"Shā-Shǔ, I know that you miss your mother. So I thought . . ." Shīfù Hui swallowed and looked down uncertainly. "When you are alone, and you need her, perhaps you can use this cloak to call your mother to you."

Apollo didn't know what to say. He desperately missed his mom. Anything that could help him feel closer to her was precious.

He lifted the cloak with one of his hands and rubbed the fine silk between his fingers.

"It would be best, though, that you don't wear it around the Temple." Shīfù Hui unbuttoned the cloak, took it off Apollo's shoulders, and folded it back up. Instructing him to hide it in his shirt.

"Would you like some tea?"

Shīfù Hui led Apollo out of the tiny bedroom and into an equally small kitchen. Where he served him a cookie and a small glass of some sort of yellowish liquid. After finishing their tea, they moved into a small front room, where Shīfù Hui read a book silently while Apollo sat down on a cushion and, after a few minutes, fell into a comfortable nap—only waking when Shīfù Hui tapped him on the shoulder informing him that it was time to return to the Temple.

Chapter Twenty-Four

If the life of the great Shā-Shǔ can teach us anything, it must be to never give up on ourselves. We may feel ordinary. We may feel unimportant. We may think that the world is moving along without us and that we are insignificant to these movements, never realizing that our own Wyvern Spirits are acting on our behalf, opening doors for us and ushering each of us toward our own destiny. Each of us has a role to play, and the world is better when we reach without fear toward it.

—The Book of the Wyvern Spirits

Apollo couldn't quite put his finger on it, but Shīfù Hui was somehow a different person outside of the school. He felt more like a friend than a teacher. He smiled more freely and often placed his hand on Apollo's shoulder or head.

After leaving Shīfù Hui's home, it took the two of them another half hour to make their way back to the Temple grounds. As they came out of the gardens and around the side of the building, Apollo noticed three adult men and an adult woman standing on the steps near the Temple's front doors.

As Apollo and Shīfù Hui got closer, these four adults began to descend the steps toward them. One of these adults called out to Shīfù Hui, sounding upset. Shīfù Hui responded in an equally irritated voice.

As these four adults continued down the steps, an older man opened the Temple doors and joined them outside. The man spoke, addressing himself to the four, who immediately turned and rushed back up the steps and into the Temple.

The man then looked at Shīfù Hui. As he spoke, Shīfù Hui's expressions changed from irritation to something more complex. He simultaneously appeared to be both afraid while also determined.

Without saying anything to Apollo, Shīfù Hui grabbed him by the arm and pulled him up the steps and back into the Temple.

They went down a hallway and through a door that led into the large central room in the middle of the school. The last time Apollo had entered this room, it had been dark, and he had been alone. However, today each of the four balconies was completely packed. As far as Apollo could tell, everyone from the village must have gathered there.

In the center of the room, a man was being held on his knees in front of Shi Ju-Long.

"Stay here, my Shā-Shŭ."

Shīfù Hui pointed to the floor and then pushed his way deeper into the crowd, leaving Apollo alone.

Apollo looked around for a moment and then noticed Ai-An. Who was also standing near the back of the crowd, not too far from where he was. She signaled for Apollo to move closer to her. It took some effort to make his way to her, but after a few minutes, they were standing side by side.

When he reached her, she looked at him doubtfully and whispered, "What are you doing here, Shā-Shǔ?"

"Shīfù Hui brought me." The answer must have satisfied her because she didn't press the point further.

"What's going on?" Apollo asked.

"The Xué in the front captured a Black Dragon. The Xué in the back is helping to guard him."

"What is a Black Dragon?"

Ai-An looked at Apollo incredulously. "You really don't know anything, do you, Shā-Shǔ."

Her accusation irritated Apollo. He knew a lot more than she thought he did. He had learned more than anyone else here realized. But as much as it embarrassed him to admit it, right now, she was right. He didn't know anything.

"A Black Dragon," Ai-An repeated herself, this time speaking more slowly as if enunciating each syllable would somehow help Apollo understand her better. "We are the White Dragons; they are Black Dragons."

"There's more than one type of dragon?" Apollo spat out in surprise.

"Of course, there is more than one type." She shook her head in disbelief, which didn't make Apollo feel any better. "We seek to protect the lotus flowers; they seek to control them."

"What is a lotus flower?"

Ai-An turned toward Apollo and tapped him on his chest. "You are a lotus flower. Now hush, I am trying to listen."

Apollo followed Ai-An's gaze toward the center of the room. He could hear one of the men in the front talking to Shi Ju-Long, but he couldn't understand him.

"Ai-An," Apollo whispered, "what is he saying?"

"He said that they caught the man leaving our village." She looked unsettled. "The Black Dragons aren't supposed to know where our villages are. It is supposed to be a secret." After another pause, she continued. "Now the Dǎoshī is asking him how he found us."

"What did he say?"

Ai-An didn't answer.

"Ai-An, what did the Black Dragon say?"

"He said that he is here for you, Shā-Shǔ. His Xué was sent, along with many others throughout China, to search every village and town until they found the American boy who had been hidden by someone named Tengfei. He said that Tengfei is the nephew of the Black Dragon's ShI-Dǎoshī."

"I know Tengfei." Apollo blurted out. "That is who brought me here. What is a ShI-Dǎoshī?"

Once again, Ai-An looked at Apollo. "The ShI-Dǎoshī is the leader over the entire Black Dragon Order. We have one too. Ours is Bái lóng hūxī. Theirs is Tan Far."

"WHAT?" Apollo nearly shouted. "Tan Far. Ling's father? He is in charge of all the Dragons?"

"No, Shā-Shǔ. You are not listening to me. We are White Dragons. We have our own ShI-Dǎoshī."

Apollo felt dizzy. It was almost too much for him to process. Tan Far, a man he had known his entire life, who had made him sandwiches when he was younger, was somehow affiliated with this place. No, wait, not this place. Ai-An had said they had their own leader. But he was nonetheless a Dragon. Did Ling know about Dragons, creeds, and cloaks?

Ai-An continued to whisper translations to Apollo, though she often fell silent for several seconds at a time.

232

"You're not translating everything."

"There are some things you do not want to hear, Shā-Shŭ."

Apollo knew he should have felt more gratitude toward Ai-An for trying to protect him, but instead, it only angered him.

"If it's about me, then I have a right to know." He snapped.

Ai-An looked at Apollo for a moment and then translated more faithfully.

"He said that Tengfei was supposed to deliver you to a Black Dragon Temple, but he betrayed Tan Far and brought you to our Temple instead. The Black Dragons have been searching for you ever since.

"The man didn't realize he had found a White Dragon village until he saw you walking outside with someone else. He recognized the gi and tattoos of the man who was with you, and he recognized you from a picture he had been given.

"He said that he would have taken you then but was uncertain of the skill level of the man who was with you. So he decided it would be safer to return to get the rest of his Xué, but was captured before he got out of the village."

Apollo thought back over his walk with Shīfù Hui. He didn't remember seeing or hearing anyone. How could so much have happened around them without the two of them even noticing?

"Now he is threatening Shi Ju-Long. He says that the rest of his Xué is still waiting for him. If Shi Ju-Long doesn't allow him to leave, then they will return to Tan Far and report the location of our village to him."

Ai-An's voice became hushed. Apollo looked at her and realized how truly frightened she was.

"He says that if the Dǎoshī wants to keep any of us alive, he must turn you over to him. If he does, then the man promises that his ShI-Dǎoshī will show the rest of us mercy. We will be allowed to join with them and become their brothers and sisters in the 'true' Dragon Order." Ai-An spoke the word *true* as though it was a disgusting thing to have to say.

As she did so, she quietly moved her body so that she was now standing just a little bit in front of Apollo.

"I won't let the Dǎoshī give you to them, Shā-Shŭ."

Apollo knew how important obedience was to his friend. Just a few months earlier, she couldn't even bring herself to disobey Lei. Now she was ready to stand with Apollo and fight against her entire village. It meant more to Apollo than he was capable of saying.

"Thank you, Ai-An, for being my friend." He reached down and took her hand in his.

A few seconds later, Ai-An breathed in relief. "The Dǎoshī said that he is not going to let them have you. He just ordered one of our Xué to execute him."

"What. They are just going to kill him?"

Apollo wasn't sure how he felt about that. Didn't they have to have a trial or something?

Ai-An responded matter-of-factly. "He doesn't want to kill him, Shā-Shŭ, but think about it. The Dǎoshī doesn't have a choice, does he? We can't guard him forever. We are a small village. If he escaped, he would tell Tan Far about our village, and then the Black Dragons would come for all of us."

As Ai-An spoke, all four members of the leading Xué gathered around their prisoner. One of them kept the man on his knees, while the other three lifted various weapons in preparation to carry out the Dǎoshī's orders. Before they could kill him, though, the Black Dragon shouted something.

The man's words drew an immediate reaction from the crowd. Some shouted in frustration while others shook their heads in disgust. The four adults who had been poised to kill the prisoner lowered their weapons and took a step back from him.

"No." Ai-An whispered.

"Why did they stop?" Apollo asked.

"He has challenged the Dǎoshī to a Shi Kiatu."

"A what?"

"An honor killing. The law says that a criminal has the right to die with honor."

"How do you die with honor?"

"By defending your life against those who are set to execute you." Ai-An answered.

"That's stupid." Apollo looked at Ai-An, wondering whether or not she was being serious. "Why would anyone allow a criminal to fight after they've already been captured?"

Ai-An looked at Apollo for a moment and then answered.

"Even criminals deserve to seek forgiveness from the Wyvern Spirits." She said, "If he wins, it means it is their will that he be allowed to go free."

"They're going to allow him to fight back against the four who are putting him to death?"

"No Shā-Shǔ, he has to fight the one who has sentenced him to die. He must fight the Dǎoshī."

"What?" Apollo asked incredulously. He looked over at Shi Ju-Long

"The Dǎoshī can't fight him. He's too old."

"He doesn't have a choice. Honor and duty require him to accept the challenge."

It didn't make any sense to Apollo. Why would anyone follow such stupid rules when they didn't have to. The Dǎoshī had hundreds of much more capable warriors standing around him.

"So they are just going to let the man kill the Dǎoshī and take me as a prisoner? Just because he shouted something?" Apollo asked, sounding skeptical.

"No. The Dǎoshī's order will remain in force. Everyone here will be honor-bound to protect you."

"But, Ai-An, if they allow him to leave, he is just going to return with more err... Black Dragons. Then they will still kill me and everyone else."

"Possibly. Or force us to join them."

Apollo repeated his protest. "That's stupid. Just kill him now?"

"Shā-Shǔ, it's our way. We must be obedient to the oaths that we have taken. Otherwise, we can't expect the Wyvern Spirits to protect us."

Apollo felt uneasy. How could allowing an older man to die and a village to get destroyed be justifiable? First, the Dǎoshī was going to be murdered in front of Apollo's eyes. Then a few days later, the Black Dragons would also attack the rest of the people in the village. Just so he could live for at most a few extra days.

As Apollo watched, the two Xué retreated to the blue balcony, leaving their prisoner unguarded and alone on the main floor with a very tired-looking Shi Ju-Long.

A moment later, a middle-aged man reached out from the balcony and handed the Black Dragon two swords. The man took these swords and then stretched out, shaking his arms and legs.

He effortlessly flipped his entire body into the air while kicking his feet out above him, landing just a few meters away from where Shi Ju-Long was standing. The Dǎoshī didn't move. Instead, he stood his ground like a statue.

The prisoner smiled and bowed to Shi Ju-Long, who returned his bow. Shi Ju-Long then reached down into two hidden pockets on either side of his pants and withdrew from each something that resembled a dragon's head. Then, with a sharp flick of his wrists, golden flames burst out of the mouths of each of these dragons and locked into place.

By the time the Black Dragon attempted his first attack, Shi Ju-Long was already blocking him. Spinning quickly to the side, Shi Ju-Long kicked the man hard in his stomach, causing him to fall backward and to the floor.

The Black Dragon stood back up and nodded toward Shi Ju-Long, still smiling. This time, he attacked with both swords out to the side, slicing inward toward the Dǎoshī's ribs. As he got closer, the Dǎoshī effortlessly turned the man's attack back onto himself by deflecting his own swords upward, cutting the Black Dragon across the sides of his face. So far, Shi Ju-Long had barely moved. Yet despite this, he was somehow winning the battle rather decidedly.

The Black Dragon must have realized that he couldn't match the Dǎoshī's skill because he changed his tactic. Instead of attacking Shi Ju-Long directly, he began to circle him, keeping himself just far enough away so that the Dǎoshī couldn't reach him, but close enough so that Shi Ju-Long would have to keep moving. This strategy proved to be far more effective. Shi Ju-Long couldn't keep up with the man's speed, and after just a few minutes of spinning around, the Dǎoshī began to get visibly tired.

The more tired he became, the slower his reactions got, allowing his assailant to draw in closer to him. Someone needed to do something.

"Why doesn't anyone help him?" Apollo looked at Ai-An.

"We can't. He is bound by his duty to fight, and we are bound by our duty not to interfere."

"Ai-An, I am not worth any of this."

"You are worth it." She looked at him intently. "But also Shā-Shŭ, this is about more than just you. We must live by our promises. If we can't remain true to ourselves during our most difficult trials, then we are without honor, and our lives are without a compass."

The Black Dragon continued darting in and out while spinning around Shi Ju-Long, who was dripping in sweat and breathing heavily.

Apollo remembered the words Lanfen had spoken to him in the kitchen. She had once told him that sometimes your duty wasn't always as straightforward as everyone else thought it was. Sometimes your destiny was to do what you knew to be right, even when everyone else thought it was wrong.

"You may have taken an oath, Ai-An, but I haven't."

With that, he let go of her hand, and yelling as loudly as he could, Apollo ran through the crowd, jumped over the railing, and then headed straight toward the assailant who was attacking Shi Ju-Long. It was stupid, and Apollo knew that it was also hopeless. He had no weapons, and he was certainly no match for the Black Dragon. As soon as he reached him, the man would just kill him.

Apollo didn't care. His life was over anyway. At least this way, his death would have some meaning.

The man turned and, for just an instant, looked at Apollo, which was all the time Shi Ju-Long needed to lunge forward and stick both of his swords through the man's chest.

By the time Apollo reached the prisoner, he was already dead. Shi Ju-Long turned toward Apollo and then nodded appreciatively.

It took Shi Ju-Long a moment to catch his breath. When he could speak again, he directed a group of four people to carry the man's body away.

Once they were gone, Shi Ju-Long gestured for Apollo to come closer to him. Speaking loudly enough for everyone in the room to hear, he asked, "Where is Jiàn Huì? Where is your caretaker?"

Shīfù Hui quickly stepped out onto the main floor and joined Apollo at his side. "I am here, Dǎoshī," Hui said, bowing his head.

"Is it true that you and young Apollo were wandering through the village today?" the Dǎoshī inquired. "I thought we had agreed that the boy was to remain in the basement."

"I'm sorry, Dǎoshī. I should have obeyed you more faithfully. Shā-Shǔ—I mean, Apollo—needed sunlight. I, er—I thought that—" Hui finished his sentence uncertainly. "I wanted to give him something."

"And how is it that the boy ended up inside our Nest?"

Once again, Shīfù Hui looked uncomfortable. "When we returned to the Temple, I brought him in here with me."

"I asked you to keep this American boy away from the sacred parts of our Temple. He shouldn't have even been allowed into our village. And now you have brought him all the way into our Nest."

Apollo watched as Shīfù Hui kept his head low.

"I am sorry, Dǎoshī. I try to follow you. I want to be better. Sometimes I am just selfish."

Hui fell to his knees. "I think that I hear the Wyvern Spirits calling me to do things, and I act when I know that I should think instead." Apollo had never heard Shīfù Hui sound so unsure of himself before.

Shi Ju-Long walked over to Shīfù Hui and put his hand on his shoulder. Then, speaking in a quieter voice, he said, "It would seem today, my dear Jiàn Hui, that you have listened to the Wyvern Spirits better than any of the rest of us. Today they have led you to save our Temple and our entire village."

Tears of relief immediately began to stream down Shīfù Hui's cheeks.

Shi Ju-Long lifted Jian Hui back to his feet and then looked up at the rest of the room, raising his voice so that everyone else would hear him.

"Jiàn Hui is a hero." The Dǎoshī bowed his head toward him. Everyone else in the room followed his example. "You have restored your family's honor. No one will ever speak your name again without great reverence."

"Thank you, Dǎoshī," Shīfù Hui mumbled, wiping his eyes.

"And you." Shi Ju-Long turned toward Apollo. "You have shown remarkable courage. You ran toward a man who you knew could kill you."

"The wings of a dragon carry them to those who are in need of his help," Apollo blurted out.

Amused and a little surprised, Shi Ju-Long inspected Apollo more closely. "Indeed they do. And we can all learn from the example you have shown us today. Today you have acted with the strength of a true Dragon. "

Apollo blurted out, "I would like to be a Dragon."

"You have the spirit of a Dragon young Apollo, and I do not doubt that in time and with the proper training, you could become a brave warrior, but unfortunately, that is not possible."

"Dǎoshī." Shīfù Hui interrupted. "There is a way Apollo could join us."

"No, Jiàn Hui, there isn't. As you well know, Dragons can only be selected from among the descendants of those who fought to protect Emperor Qin Shi Huang. It is an absolute law. No outsider has ever been permitted to train as a Dragon."

"Dǎoshī, forgive me, but you said yourself that the boy has shown the courage of a Dragon and that he has the spirit of a Dragon."

"Yes, Hui, but he does not have the heritage or the lineage of a Dragon."

"Then I'll adopt him."

"The boy has a father already." Shi Ju-Long waved dismissively.

"A boy can have two fathers. No law says otherwise."

Shi Ju-Long remained silent while he considered Jiàn Hui's words. Then, after a few seconds, he smiled. "I have to concede your point. I know of no law that says a boy cannot have two fathers."

He turned to look at Apollo. "To the rest of the world, you will continue to be known as Apollo Salvatoir. But to us, you will now be known as Jiàn Shā-Shǔ. To us, Shā-Shǔ, you will be the son of Jiàn Hui."

Apollo felt himself being engulfed in Shīfù Hui's arms.

"My son, my boy."

Apollo couldn't remember a time when his birth father had ever hugged him like that or showed him any kind of affection at all. Shīfù Hui had become more like a father to Apollo than William Salvatoir had ever been. Apollo lifted his arms and returned Shīfù Hui's hug.

"I am afraid, Hui, that you are celebrating a little too early. The boy must still pass the Lóng Tiǎozhàn, just like everyone else."

"Yes, Dǎoshī. We will work hard together over the summer to prepare."

"No, I think not. He must take the test now. And not just the Lóng Tiǎozhàn for Blue Engrows. Apollo is almost twelve years old. Next year, the children his age will begin training as Orange Poppies. I am sorry, Hui, but he must show that he can perform the Lóng Tiǎozhàn at their level."

In an instant, Shīfù Hui's expression changed from joy to defeat. "Dǎoshī, it takes years to prepare for the Lóng Tiǎozhàn. My son doesn't even know what he is supposed to do."

"I am sorry, Hui, but I have stretched the rules rather far in allowing you to adopt him. Many Dragon descendants in the village will never get the opportunity to train. No matter how much courage he may have displayed today, it wouldn't be right for me to allow him to train unless he can pass the same Lóng Tiǎozhàn as everyone else. If the Wyvern Spirits will it, then the boy will pass. If not, then he can return to the village, and I will assign the two of you to work in any profession that you choose."

Shīfù Hui reluctantly allowed Shi Ju-Long to lead him away from his newly adopted son and out toward the blue balcony, leaving Apollo alone in the middle of the central floor. Every eye in the Nest now watched him intently.

Shīfù Hui was right. Apollo had absolutely no idea what they expected him to do. He didn't even know what a Lóng Tiǎozhàn was. All he could think of was the Dragon's Creed. Or at least, those parts of it that he had already learned.

Embarrassed and feeling awkward, Apollo shouted as loudly as he could.

"The feet of a dragon stand firm against evil, walking toward and never away from duty.

"The, um—wings of a dragon carry him to those who are in need of his, er—help.

"And The head of a dragon must seek learning and knowledge throughout its entire life."

Apollo paused and looked around the room. Other than a random cough from one of the balconies, no one said anything or gave any signs whether or not he had done the right thing. Instead, they all just kept staring at him, making Apollo feel very uncomfortable.

He took a deep breath and briefly considered doing a gymnastics routine for them. It might not be what they were expecting, but it would certainly be a heck of a way to go down in flames. There was enough space on the main floor for him to show off his tumbling skills.

Thinking about gymnastics gave Apollo another idea, though. He reached into his shirt and pulled out the dragon cloak that Shīfù Hui had given him. Unfolding it, Apollo put it around his shoulders and fastened the button under his neck. Then, with the cloak secured around his body, he silently prayed for his mother's help.

Apollo looked around the room again, took another deep breath, and then began to execute each of the forms he had learned during his secret practice sessions down in the basement. At first, he felt silly, but then his muscle memory took over, and he fell into a rhythm.

It took Apollo about twenty minutes to complete all the forms he had learned. When he was done, he stood up straight again, turned toward the Dǎoshī, and bowed. The entire room burst into applause as Shi Ju-Long nodded his head back toward Apollo.

The Dǎoshī walked out into the center of the room, took Apollo by the hand, and lifted his arm high above his head, shouting, "Shā-Shǔ, the Dragon."

Everyone in the room repeated the chant together, "Shā-Shǔ, the Dragon."

The Dǎoshī then looked down at Apollo and spoke to him again. "Very impressive, Shā-Shǔ. You will take the place of Jiàn Huì's other son and your brother. Which means that you will train with Lei, Fānyì, and Ai-An. With you joining them, their Xué will once again be complete."

Over the next several minutes, almost everyone in the room came down to personally congratulate Apollo and welcome him into the Temple. As a result, he had to remain in the Dragon's Nest until everyone else had left. When he finished bowing to the last person, Apollo looked around and found Ai-An, Fānyì, and Lei waiting for him near one of the doors. Apollo walked over and joined them.

"I think I need a nap," Apollo muttered. Then, uncertain whether or not that was allowed, he looked at Lei. "Can I go down to my room for a little while?"

"Shā-Shǔ, you don't sleep down there anymore. You sleep upstairs with us."

The three of them led Apollo through the archway that led into the blue training room and from there down one of the side hallways—stopping in front of a closed door.

"This is your room, Shā-Shǔ." Lei opened the door and led Apollo inside. The room was bright and clean. It wasn't much bigger than the one in the basement, but Apollo was relieved to see that it had two large windows that looked out over the gardens. He could see the sky, trees, grass, and the pond full of large goldfish.

Apollo looked at Lei and bowed. "I need to go and get a few things out of my old room. Would that be okay?"

Lei nodded and ordered Ai-An to accompany him.

As soon as they were alone, Ai-An reached down and grabbed Apollo's hand. Then, the two of them walked to the basement together. Once there, Apollo collected the coin Ling had given him and the blue book from Shīfù Hui, after which they returned back upstairs.

When Apollo opened the door to his new room, a blue robe was waiting for him on a chair in the corner. Apollo removed his plain white shirt and proudly replaced it with the blue robe. Then, after a short nap, Apollo left his room and returned to the Blue Engrow training room, where the rest of his new Xué was waiting for him.

As he crossed the room, Lei looked at Apollo's arm and smirked. "Now the fun part, my new friend. It's time to see how much pain you can endure. You need to visit the Wénshēn yìshùjiā."

"The what?" Apollo asked nervously.

"The tattoo artist," Ai-An giggled. "You have earned your dragon, but he isn't on your arm yet." With that, they led Apollo out a door and into another part of the Temple, where Apollo had never ventured.

Chapter Twenty-Five

The great Shā-Shŭ is reported to have once stated that he admired courage above all else. Indeed, in the Lìshĭ scrolls of Daletezhen, he wrote the following tribute of Tengfei:

"When others wanted to run from their duty, it was the firmness of Tengfei's resolve and the fierceness of his bravery that pressed valor into the hearts of his allies and fear into the hearts of his foes."

Such a stirring memorial written by the very hand of the man whose name is now synonymous with courage can leave no one in doubt of the bold and fearless nature of the man who gave his life to protect the young Shā-Shŭ.

—The Book of the Wyvern Spirits

Tengfei had spent his entire life in the service of his people. Throughout his childhood, his parents taught him to love their traditions and respect their great leaders.

As a young man, Tengfei idolized his uncle. Everyone spoke of his goodness, his wisdom, and his power. They talked about how he was the greatest ShI-Dǎoshī in history and how he would one day restore peace throughout the world.

With so much to live up to, Tengfei worked hard to be worthy of his family's heritage. He trained with purpose and determination. His commitment inspired the rest of his Xué, lifting them above everyone else. Within their tiny village of Xitanxiang, no other Xué of his age group could defeat them in the Dragon's Nest. When they eventually completed their training at the age of twenty-four, they quickly established themselves as not just the best Xué of their age or even the best of their village. Soon they had gained a reputation for being the most effective Xué in the entire Order.

This success brought the four of them tremendous honor and recognition. It wasn't long before their fame also brought them to the attention of the ShI-Dǎoshī himself. As a result, Tengfei was invited to spend an evening with the ShI-Dǎoshī in his home.

Initially, the experience had lived up to his expectations. His uncle appeared gracious, kind, thoughtful, and strong. In time, though, as Tengfei had many similar opportunities to associate with Tan Far, he got to know the man much better. It was these later interactions that ultimately led to Tengfei's disillusionment.

His time with the ShI-Dǎoshī revealed some unsettling truths about his uncle. He was clever, but he wasn't wise. He wasted lives and resources, often unnecessarily, just to make the smallest of gains. He was also selfish and vengeful. At times he could even be cruel.

The thing that most bothered Tengfei, though, was that Tan Far had lied to his followers by keeping a great secret from them, which was that there was another Dragon Order. All his life, Tengfei had been taught that their institution was singular. He had always believed that they alone had descended from the original guards of Emperor Qin Shi Huang and that it was their responsibility to protect his authority to rule China. From his childhood, Tengfei had committed himself to this conviction, all the while having no idea that there was another group who shared the same heritage, traditions, and legacy.

In time, Tengfei learned that the other order distinguished between the two by adding colors to their names. According to this tradition, the other order referred to themselves as the White Dragons, while they called members of his order Black Dragons, though that wasn't how Tan Far referred to them. Instead, he called their own order simply the Dragons while referring to the others as "Lost Dragons."

When Tengfei asked his uncle why he had kept knowledge of the Lost Dragons from the people, Tan Far responded by telling him that if others knew about their existence, they might become corrupt. According to his uncle, only his most loyal Xué could be entrusted with such dangerous information.

In many ways, Tan Far hadn't been wrong. The knowledge of another Dragon Order did begin to corrupt Tengfei, though he viewed this corruption as having saved his soul.

In time, Tengfei and his friend Niu, who had also trained with him in the same Leheqi, found an opportunity to meet with Bái lóng hūxī, the ShI-Dǎoshī of the other Dragon Order. Bái lóng hūxī was everything that Tan Far had not been. He was sincere, quiet, thoughtful, and compassionate.

Before their meeting had ended, both Tengfei and Niu had sworn an oath of allegiance to the White Dragons. However, Bái lóng hūxī ordered them to remain in the service of Tan Far so that they could periodically report his plans back to their new ShI-Dǎoshī.

When Tan Far ordered the death of Tayleigh Salvatoir, it had been Tengfei who had warned her of the plot on her life and who tried to help her escape. When his uncle later ordered him to have Apollo Salvatoir delivered to the Temple in the village of Jia Quiaogou, Tengfei chose to make the most important sacrifice of his life. One that he knew would change his circumstances forever since there was no way such a direct betrayal could be concealed from his uncle.

Instead of following his uncle's orders, Tengfei delivered the boy to the White Dragon village of Daletezhen and then went into hiding.

Tengfei would never again be allowed to return to his home, and his name would be viewed with dishonor and shame by his friends and relatives.

Tengfei's sacrifice also meant that he would never again see his wife or hold his baby daughter. His newly born little girl would grow up being told that her father was a traitor. She would carry that mark on her throughout the rest of her life. The daughter of a traitor might as well be a traitor herself.

However, Tengfei knew that some things mattered more than himself or his family. His actions would help keep the American boy alive, which would also protect the lives of many thousands of others. Perhaps even millions.

After going into hiding, Tengfei remained at the residence of Bái lóng hūxī, only leaving occasionally to meet up with Niu so that the two of them could exchange intelligence.

During his last such excursion, as Tengfei traveled to their agreed-upon meeting place, he fell into a well-laid trap that had been set for him by the three remaining members of his own former Xué and was captured.

When Tengfei betrayed Tan Far, he didn't just bring dishonor to himself. He also brought the same disgrace to the other members of his Xué, which meant that they too would have to pay the same price he did. As a result, Tan Far exiled them from the Order, telling them that they would only be allowed to return to their families if they first restored their honor by bringing Tengfei to him.

After capturing and securing him, they held Tengfei prisoner for a short time in Jia Quiaogou while they waited for further instructions from the Shi-Dǎoshī. These instructions were delivered by another Xué. Led by a man named Shun. Shun explained that the seven of them were to guard Tengfei as they traveled together from Jia Quiaogou aboard a cargo ship headed to the United States.

Since arriving at the Embarcadero in San Francisco three weeks earlier, Tengfei had been kept in a tiny prison cell in the basement of the Skinny Pig Grill. Where he had been given very little water and absolutely nothing to eat during his stay there. It was late on the twenty-fourth night of his captivity in that cell when Shun, and the members of Tengfei's former Xué, entered the basement to collect him.

"Your uncle wants that we to bring you upstairs."

As Shun opened the cell door, the other three prepared to grab him. A precaution that turned out not to be necessary. Tengfei was too weak to put up any kind of a fight. He could barely even stand. They ended up having to carry him up the stairs.

Tengfei knew he was going to die and that it was unlikely to be a quick death. So he decided that he might as well win a few victories along the way by taunting his captors before they killed him.

"Hey, Huang. I bet you can't wait to see your wife. But, before you kiss her, make sure you wash your hands. You wouldn't want to get my blood on her apron."

"You are getting what you deserve." Huang spat back.

"What about you, Lihua? We have fought side by side since childhood. You used to have a crush on me. Now you get to help murder me. That must be a fun way to spend the evening." She looked away from him and didn't respond.

Tengfei continued. Now speaking to all of them, "When my daughter is old enough, will you do me a favor? Will you tell her that it was you who slaughtered her daddy? Oh, and be sure to tell her how cowardly you all were. Let her know that it took five of you and that even then, you still had to wait until after I was too weak to defend myself."

As they entered a room at the back of the deli, Tengfei caught sight of his uncle standing near a long stainless steel table. There was an assortment of knives and other cutlery on the wall next to him.

Doing his best to speak English, Shun addressed Tan Far. "We have bring you the young man, as you tell us."

"Thank you, Shun." Tan Far then looked at the three members of Tengfei's Xué. "You have almost completely restored your honor. You have only one thing left to do. You will help me dispose of this traitor. Remove his clothes and tie him down to the table."

Chapter Twenty-Six

The maple tree gives no thought to how large it will grow or how far its branches will extend. It simply does the best it can each day to stretch itself a little farther and reach a little higher. If its shade eventually covers and protects the entire earth, it is not because of a single action but rather due to a lifetime of patient effort.

—The Book of the Wyvern Spirits

The week following Apollo's exhibition in the Nest was unlike anything he had ever experienced before. Everywhere he went, people regarded him with admiration. He was being treated like a hero even though his part in what had happened had been pretty small.

In the Nest, the Dǎoshī had told everyone that they should all aspire to be more like him, and so that was precisely what everyone was now obediently trying to do.

The attention made Apollo uncomfortable, but he was at least happy again. He had friends, he had a caring father, and he even had a grandmother. Lanfen now insisted that Apollo call her his Năinai.

He was also now free to go anywhere he wanted, as long as he remained with his Xué. Except, of course, at night, when they all separated into their bedrooms. His room was airy, bright, and clean. He had a chair, a desk, and a small cabinet where he could put his clothes and other belongings.

The training season was almost over. Which meant he wouldn't get to keep this room for very long. When they all returned to the Temple after their summer break, his Xué would ascend to the Orange Poppy Leheqi, where they would be assigned new rooms on the second floor. But that was okay. Any bedroom would be better than the one in the basement where he lived for the past year.

On the last day of training, he was visited by the Dăoshī, who entered his room and sat down on the chair near Apollo's desk. Shi Ju-Long invited Apollo to sit down on his mat, a request which Apollo immediately obeyed.

After a few moments of silence, in which the Dăoshī admired the view of the gardens through one of Apollo's windows, the old man looked down and began to speak.

"Now that you are a Dragon, Shā-Shŭ, there are many things that you do not know. Things that all of the other children have grown up learning and take for granted. You have a difficult task ahead of you."

"I will work hard, Dăoshī."

"I trust that you will. I will leave it to your father to instruct you in most of our traditions. But there are a few things that he does not know and that he doesn't need to know, but that you will have to be aware of if you are going to remain alive." Shi Ju-Long looked at Apollo sternly. "What I am going to tell you must not be shared with anyone else. Not with your new father, nor with any member of your Xué. Do you understand, Shā-Shŭ?"

Apollo nodded.

"This is not a directive that you can take lightly. I must have your absolute word that you will never divulge what I now tell you to anyone, under any circumstances."

Apollo again nodded and this time said, "Yes, Dǎoshī, I promise."

"Good, Shā-Shŭ. I believe you. I believe that you are capable of keeping your word." Shi Ju-Long shifted his balance slightly and looked out through one of Apollo's windows again.

"Things are not always as they seem. For example, you see our beautiful gardens?" Shi Ju-Long looked back at Apollo. "What do you suppose would happen to those gardens if we stopped taking care of them?" He waited for Apollo to answer.

"They would die?" Apollo answered uncertainly.

"Eventually, yes, I think they would. They would survive for a while, but eventually, the wild parts of the wilderness would creep in and strangle out the tender and more beautiful plants that we have chosen to cultivate here. The fish would, of course, die quickly without us feeding them. And even the lotus flowers in the bottom of the pond would eventually cease to bloom.

"It is our job, Shā-Shŭ, to care for the garden. As Dragons, we are the world's caretakers, or gardeners, if you will. As gardeners, we sometimes have to prune back the wild things that threaten to overtake the garden so that civilizations can continue to flourish.

"Unfortunately, as you saw the other day, there is more than one type of Dragon in the world. We are the White Dragons. We call the others the Black Dragons. Both orders descend from the same roots. Both of us come from the original Order of the Dragons. But they split away from us many hundreds of years ago.

"During most of the centuries that have followed, the Black Dragons have been significantly less powerful than us. The strength of our order allowed us to keep them in check easily. However, Shā-Shŭ, things have changed. Gradually, and without anyone realizing that it was happening, the Black Dragons grew in strength while we dwindled. Sadly, today the garden has become overrun with wild things."

Apollo nodded, though he wasn't sure he understood anything Shi Ju-Long was saying.

"Today, there are only three White Dragon villages left. The others have either been destroyed or have joined themselves to the Black Dragons." Shi Ju-Long's voice sounded heavy.

He looked down at Apollo. "If it hadn't been for your courage the other day, they would have destroyed our village as well. Then the White Dragons would be left with only two villages. Thankfully, though, Shā-Shŭ, you listened to the Wyvern Spirits, and at least for now, you helped to spare us from that fate."

Looking up at Shi Ju-Long, Apollo asked, "Dǎoshī, what about the other members of the prisoner's Xué? Won't they still return and tell Tan Far where we are?"

"That is a very thoughtful question." Shi Ju-Long looked genuinely impressed.

"After our Shi Kiatu the other day, I sent out two of our most capable Xué to track down and destroy the remaining three members of the Black Dragon Xué." The Dǎoshi breathed out heavily.

"Were they all killed?"

"Yes, they were, and their deaths have ensured that the location of our village and Temple will remain a secret. But that safety rests on the edge of a blade of grass. It can topple so easily. And Shā-Shǔ, I am afraid that you are the key to keeping that balance steady."

"What do you mean, I am the key?"

Shi Ju-Long once again exhaled. This time more slowly. "You have a friend named Tan Ling, correct?"

Apollo nodded affirmatively.

"Her father is the ShI-Dǎoshī of the Black Dragons. I'm afraid, Shā-Shǔ, that your friendship with the girl was not accidental. It was a part of a plan or trap, which Tan Far devised to ensnare you and your parents."

The Dǎoshī's words momentarily stung Apollo. What did he mean, Ling's friendship had only been part of a trap? Apollo considered his words but then realized that they couldn't be true. At least not entirely. There was just too much sincerity in his friendship with Ling for her to have been pretending.

Perhaps sensing his doubt, Shi Ju-Long added, "I do not know if Ling was aware of the plan. She may have been just as much a victim as you were. Regardless, Tan Far did put her in your path so that he could get to your err… American father."

"Why would the ShI-Dǎoshī of the Black Dragons care so much about my family?"

"Your father is a very wealthy and powerful man, Shā-Shǔ. If Tan Far were able to get his hands on your father's money, it would give him access to almost unlimited resources. He could use your wealth to track down the three remaining White Dragon Temples. The wild things would then be free to choke the life out of the rest of the garden. As a result, the world would descend that much closer toward chaos. This is why Tan Far instructed Tengfei to bring you to China."

"That is something I don't understand, Dǎoshī. I thought my father and his assistant decided to send me here."

"Yes and no. From what I have gathered, your American father wanted to send you away to a private school ever since you were a toddler. However, your mother refused to allow this. After her death, Tan Far convinced your father to send you to what your father believed was a school in China. Tan Far planned to keep you as a prisoner there until he was ready to have you killed."

Apollo looked at Shi Ju-Long incredulously. "Why does Tan Far want to kill me?"

"Think about it, Shā-Shǔ. Once your parents were both dead, you would inherit all of their money. If Tan Far controlled you, it would be very easy for him to also take control of your inheritance. Had we not intercepted you, you would already be dead.

"Tan Far entrusted his nephew, Tengfei, with the task of delivering you to the Black Dragons. Unhappily for Tan Far, but fortunately for the rest of us, Tengfei had long ago sworn an oath to our order. Given how important it was to keep you alive and out of the hands of Tan Far, Tengfei brought you here to us instead."

"But if Tengfei worked for you, then why did he abandon me at the airport? Why didn't he bring me all the way to the Temple?"

Shi Ju-Long looked unsettled. "That was an unfortunate and almost unforgivable mistake on the part of Tengfei. He was supposed to accompany you here and then go into hiding. However, when your airplane landed on the abandoned airstrip outside our village, Tengfei had fallen asleep. While he slept, your father's assistant used the opportunity to leave you on the airstrip by yourself." Shi Ju-Long replied.

"Though in fairness to her, Tengfei did tell her that he had arranged for transportation for the two of you from the airport. I don't think she realized how vulnerable she had left you."

Apollo turned his head so that he could see Shi Ju-Long better.

"Won't Tan Far just ask Jamie where she brought me?"

"That is a risk, yes. But we have gone to great lengths to make sure this doesn't happen. Tengfei told Tan Far that he would send you to China using commercial airlines. He even booked airfare in your names, though obviously, the people who ended up using those tickets weren't the two of you."

Shi Ju-Long stood up and began slowly pacing around the room.

"We didn't want to use commercial airlines because they are too easy to track. We felt that our safest option was to use a private jet. By then, your father had cut off all contact with Tan Far, and we hoped that it wouldn't occur to him that we would send you to China that way."

"It wasn't until several weeks after your arrival that we found out what had happened. When you showed up on our doorstep alone, we didn't know what to think. All we could do that night was continue with the plan and keep you hidden safely in our basement."

Apollo looked down at his feet uncomfortably.

"Shīfù, you should send me back to California. I have brought you too much trouble."

"That, Shā-Shǔ, is the reason that I came to talk to you, and the primary thing that I need for you to understand. I am afraid that you will probably never be able to return to California. If you do, it won't be for many years. The only place where you are safe is here." Shi Ju-Long waited to give Apollo time to process his words.

Apollo kept his eyes on his feet. "If you sent me back, then you would all be safer." Apollo then looked up, and his voice broke as he continued, "Tan Far might get me, but at least he would leave the rest of our village alone."

"No, my boy. If we were to send you back, then you would be killed, and so would we. If Tan Far got ahold of your money, it would likely tip the scales irrevocably in his favor. Remember, Shā-Shǔ; everything rests on a blade of grass. If that balance topples, it will be only a matter of time before Tan Far brings about the end of us all.

"I need to know that you understand this." The Dǎoshī again paused and looked intently into Apollo's eyes. "I need to know that you understand why you must always remain here with us. More than just your life depends on it."

Apollo managed to nod.

"Good. Then you will write to your American father, telling him that you would prefer to stay here with us for the summer. Don't mention any names or share details about your training, the weather, the animals, or anything else someone might use to track you down. Simply tell him that the school has invited you to stay. I will make sure it is delivered to him."

Apollo nodded again and then asked, "Does this mean that I will be spending the summer here in the Temple?"

"No, Jiàn Shā-Shǔ, you get to go home. Just not to your American home. You are a member of our village. You will spend the summer in the home of your father, Jiàn Hui."

Shi Ju-Long was about to leave but instead returned to his seat.

"You have listened to me very faithfully. Before I go, is there anything you would like to know? I think that you have earned the right to ask a few questions."

Apollo hesitated, searching his mind. Of course, anything he asked would feel frivolous after the weight of what they had just discussed. But as he thought about it, there were still a few things he didn't understand. So long as the Dǎoshī was willing to answer him, Apollo wasn't going to miss the opportunity.

"What is a lotus flower?"

Shi Ju-Long smiled broadly at him. "Ah, well, that is an easy question. A lotus flower is a small pink-and-white plant that blooms in our ponds." He laughed, pointing out the window toward the garden. "But I suppose you are wondering more about the symbolism and not the plant?"

Apollo nodded.

"The lotus flower is unique to all of nature. The white-and-pink petals rise out of the water toward the sunlight, beautiful, clean, and strong each morning. Then at night, the blossoms pull back and retract down into the muddy floor of the pond. This cycle of constant rebirth mirrors what we see in humanity, both among individuals and also the nations they inhabit.

"Individuals are sometimes stretching up toward the sun. Other times they are retracting down into the mud. But Shā-Shǔ, they never remain in the dirt forever. They always rise again. When they do, they shake off all traces of their former life in the dirt and glow brightly and beautifully once again.

"The lotus flowers represent the people of the world. As Dragons, we are sworn to protect both them and their civilizations. Everything we do here in the Temple is to prepare us for that purpose." Shi Ju-Long seemed to be enjoying their discussion much more now.

"Can you tell me the rest of the Dragon's Creed? I know what the feet, the wings, and the head do, but I don't know anything else."

"Ah, yes. You have certainly already proven yourself when it comes to the final precept of the Dragon's Creed. You did so the other day when you ran out into the nest toward certain death. It is simply this: *'The fire of a dragon is used to destroy evil and to defend good.'*"

"How do Dragons—er, I mean, how do we make fire?"

"Well, Shā-Shǔ, a Dragon uses many different types of fire. It might be your hands, your mind, or your talents. Sometimes, as you have already seen, after all else has failed, it might also be your weapons. Dragons must use these tools to defend all that is right in this world, and never to enrich or empower themselves."

With that, Shi Ju-Long stood up and began walking toward the door.

"Now, my dear boy, work hard over the summer. Prepare yourself to return in the autumn. I look forward to watching you grow, Jiàn Shā-Shǔ."

Shi Ju-Long bowed his head toward Apollo and then left him alone with his thoughts.

THE END

Hiram James Bertoch

A personal note from the author:

Thank you for the privilege of sharing the opening book of the Apollo and Ling Saga with you! I hope that you enjoyed reading their adventure as much as I have enjoyed writing it. Apollo and Ling have lived in my heart for many decades. Ever since I was ten years old. For information about future book releases, or to read details not shared in the books, as well as short stories that I have written from the world of Apollo and Ling, visit my website!

www.ApolloSalvatoir.com

Finally, a quick comment about the nature of publishing these books. As an indie author I am not supported by a big publishing company. If you enjoyed my story, I would be profoundly grateful to you if you would consider helping others to discover the Apollo and Ling Saga by recommending my books to a friend.

Things that help a lot!

Honest reviews online!

Recommending this book to your friends both online and in person!

Above all though, thank you with all my heart for reading my stories!

Made in the USA
Middletown, DE
06 March 2022